Kinma

Brackenbelly

And the
Dragon Duct Forest

Also Available

Brackenbelly
and the
Beast of Hogg-Bottom Farm

Brackenbelly
and the Horror of the
Harvest Moon

Time Guardians:
The Minotaur's Eclipse
The Mini Missions
The Centaur's Eclipse

Rogue Racer

Moggy on a Mission

Star Friend

The Night I Helped Santa

The Magic Smile

Kinmaran Chronicles II

Brackenbelly

And the
Dragon Duct Forest

Gareth Baker

Illustrated by Vicky Kuhn

First published in Kindle 2013.
In paperback by Taralyn Books/Lulu July 2013.
This revised edition published June 2019

3rd Edition
© Gareth Baker 2019

Cover art and character sketches by Vicky Kuhn
Vickykuhn.com

ISBN-13:
978-1717189059

ISBN-10:
1717189059

For William

The Characters of Kinmara and What's Gone Before

Isomee

Isomee has lived with her uncle for almost as long as she can remember and didn't realise he treated her badly. She loves nature, especially her chostri on the farm, but she longs to explore the world.

Brackenbelly

Brackenbelly is an uma warrior with an amazing power and a kind heart. He befriended Isomee, but left her behind on Hogg-Bottom farm thinking she would be safe from her cruel uncle.

Uncle Hogg-Bottom

Uncle Hogg-Bottom has treated Isomee like a slave ever since she came to live with him. He is cruel and lazy but it seems that Brackenbelly has made him change his ways.

Bramble and Thorn

Bramble and Thorn are two of Isomee's chostri. Brackenbelly bought Bramble. Thorn is Isomee's favourite. Very fast runners, chostri are brave and resourceful.

Brackenbelly's Pack

Made from an incredible fabric that won't burn,
Brackenbelly's pack rolls up into a handy bundle that
can be worn across his back.

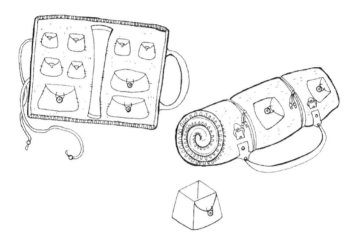

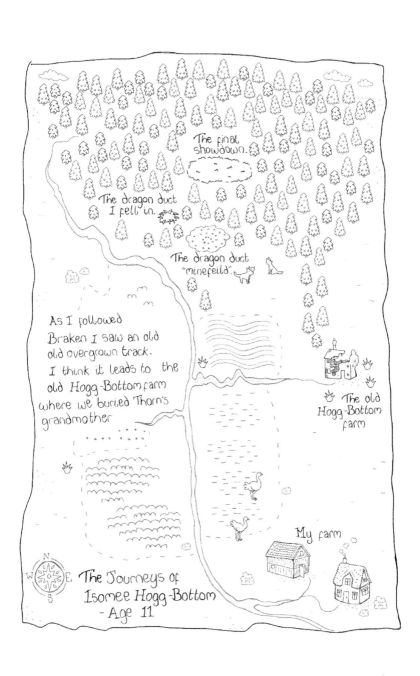

The final showdown.

The dragon duct I fell in.

The dragon duct "minefeild".

As I followed Braken I saw an old old overgrown track.
I think it leads to the old Hogg-Bottom farm where we buried Thorn's grandmother

The old Hogg-Bottom farm

My farm

The Journeys of Isomee Hogg-Bottom
- Age 11

One

The wind howled like a feral chostri, but Isomee was

determined to carry on climbing.

Her uma friend, Brackenbelly, was a just little

further up the mountain. His strong muscles made it

easier for him to lift himself from rock to rock and

swing from crag to crag.

His grey skin was almost white with cold.

Isomee's didn't have much more colour.

Climbing the mountain was harder than she'd expected, but Isomee knew she was almost at the top. And once they were there, she would be free — really free — for the first time ever.

Isomee looked up just as Brackenbelly scrambled over the top of the mountain and disappeared from view.

She took a lungful of cold air and prepared to reach for the final handhold. She stretched up, but it was just out of reach.

"Brackenbelly?" Isomee called, but all she heard in return was the screech of the wind as it whistled past, trying to pluck her off the rock face. She called again, louder this time, but still no answer came.

"I can do this," Isomee said to herself, sending great billows of hot breath out of her mouth. The warm air chilled around her fingers. "If I can just stretch a little bit more, I can reach it. I know I can."

She extended her arm again, but the rock was just too far to reach.

"I'm *not* going to give up now that I'm so close."

She looked at the crack in the gritty rock she was trying to reach. It wasn't that far. Maybe she could try…

Isomee bent her knees and got ready to try her idea.

She jumped.

Her fingertips brushed the top of the rock she was aiming for…

And missed.

She had just enough time to scream, "Brackenbelly!"

And then she fell.

A tug on her arm stopped her falling.

"Got you," Brackenbelly said in his deep, gravelly voice.

Isomee looked up into his large eyes. He was kneeling at the top of the mountain, his strong hand gripping her wrist, his long hair whipping in the air. She wrapped her fingers around his forearm and then grabbed his other hand.

"I'm going to pull you up," Brackenbelly said. "When you get up here, get ready to be amazed."

Isomee felt herself rise into the air as Brackenbelly stood up and pulled her back onto firm ground. She let go of his wrists and threw herself at him.

"Thank you," she said.

"You're welcome," Brackenbelly said, his words as stiff as his body.

"Wow!" Isomee said, letting go of him.

From the top of the mountain, it felt like Isomee could see the whole of Kinmara. After a lifetime of living on a tiny farm, the world before her seemed to go on and on and on.

It was all laid out in front of her, just waiting for Brackenbelly to show her.

In the distance, she could see another range of mountains. There were wide rivers that travelled across the land like silvery snakes. There were deep, green forests. Tiny dots moved around on the ground and in the sky. And then there were the cities that seemed to wink and sparkle at her in the bright sunshine. Her whole life was ahead of her — she only had to reach out and take it.

"This is just a-mazing!" Isomee said, a huge smile on her face. The difficult climb *had* been worth it.

"This is just the beginning."

Isomee hopped from foot to foot with excitement. She stepped forward, keen to start her adventures.

"Isomee! Look out!" Brackenbelly called, but it was too late.

Before she had a chance to stop herself, Isomee slipped on the snow-covered rocks beneath her feet. She landed flat on her back and went sliding down a chute of ice.

Down and down she went, all the time gathering speed. Faster and faster she went until she flew over the edge of the mountain and out into the sky.

"Brackenbelly!" she screamed, but the words were swallowed up as she fell. Her dress tangled around her. Her curly, red hair flapped in her face. She was falling and there was nothing to stop her.

Nothing at all.

Not this time.

Isomee's fall came to a halt when she plunged down into a pool of water. She sank to the bottom. The water was warm and comforting. She could have stayed there forever enjoying its friendly embrace. Then she remembered she needed to breathe.

She swam back up, her arms and legs working furiously. When she broke the surface, Isomee gasped for breath.

Once her breathing was back to normal and she felt safe, she swept her hair out of her face and looked around.

She was in the middle of a lake, not far from the bank. The land that surrounded the water was covered in plants. There were tall trees, flowers and bushes, all bursting with colour and life. Small birds with long beaks flew up to them and put their heads inside. Various bird songs and calls filled the air. Above her, the sun was bright and hot.

"Issssssomeeeee!"

She looked up.

Brackenbelly was tumbling through the air towards her. She'd forgotten all about him because the oasis was so beautiful.

6

Isomee had just enough time to move out of the way when, *ker-splash*, Brackenbelly landed in the water beside her. A few moments later, he burst through the surface and, just like she had, took an enormous breath.

"That was fun," he said, the smile on his face exposing his fangs. His long, black hair had come out of its neat top-knot and flowed around his shoulders.

"I thought I was going to die," Isomee confessed.

"Did you?' Brackenbelly said.

"Yes."

'Oh dear. That might be a problem. The world of adventure is dangerous, Isomee. Perhaps, if you're not ready to join me on my journeys, you should go back to your uncle."

"No, that's not what I meant," she said, panicking at Brackenbelly's sudden change in attitude. She couldn't go back. She really couldn't.

"I'm not so sure. You've nearly died twice already. I think it's best you go back home."

"No, please," Isomee said, hearing her own desperation.

"No, Isomee. I've made a mistake. You can't come with me. It's best you stay here, in your bed."

"What? I'm not in bed."

Isomee looked around her, checking she was right and he was wrong.

"Yes, you are," Brackenbelly said. "Can't you hear your uncle calling? You'd better wake up, or you'll be in trouble."

"No, this can't be happening. Please don't leave me. Please!"

"I'm sorry, Isomee, it's for your own good."

"Brackenbelly, don't go. Don't..."

Two

"...Go!" Isomee screamed, sitting up in bed. Her heart was beating so fast she could see her chest moving through her grey, tatty dress.

She looked around her tiny, empty room. The only thing in it was the mattress of straw and chostri feathers that she laid on. She didn't need cupboard for clothes or toys. She had none to put away — just a few belongings she hung on the back of the door. Belongings that Brackenbelly had given her yesterday.

It had been a dream. Just a dream.

Except not all of it was unreal and untrue. Brackenbelly had left her behind, only not in some beautiful garden, but at the front door. It was hard to believe that it had only happened yesterday.

There was a knock at the door.

"Good morning, Isomee. Are you all right? I thought I heard you call out," Uncle Hogg-Bottom said, popping his head around the bedroom door. He was already dressed in his working clothes. He'd even brushed his hair and beard.

"I'm all right," she said, smiling at her uncle. It wasn't because she was happy to see him, though.

Ever since Brackenbelly had left, her uncle had been acting strangely. He'd even said he was sorry she'd lost her best friend. Then he'd said she could take the day off all her chores around the farm and house. He'd even cooked her a meal. It was burnt and it tasted horrible, but at least he'd tried.

At first, she'd found it hard to accept that he was being so nice to her, but to her surprise, it seemed genuine. She hoped he was going to carry on being nice to her today, too.

"Shall we go to the market today, like we talked about?" he asked.

Isomee looked across at him, barely able to hide her surprise. She'd wanted to go to the market for years, but her uncle never let her leave the farm.

She'd been amazed when her uncle had suggested it yesterday. He hadn't been to Kilmiston market for a long time because they had no money, but when Brackenbelly had visited the farm he had bought a chostri, the giant birds she and her uncle bred.

Brackenbelly had paid a poor price for Bramble, the chostri he'd chosen, considering he'd also solved the mystery of the beast of Hogg-Bottom farm as part of the deal. In fact, her uncle had tricked him, and for some reason, Isomee hadn't warned him.

In the end, Brackenbelly had ridden off on his new ride with a special halter she'd designed for chostri. Even though she wanted to leave with him, she knew she had to remain on the farm. One day it would be hers again. And she had big plans.

"Can I really come with you?" Isomee asked.

"I've been thinking about what you were saying the other day. You should see how the market works. As you get older you'll need to go there by yourself."

"We do need to go," Isomee said. "The larder's almost bare."

"Good. Let's cook breakfast together and then we can make plans. Don't be long."

He left the room and Isomee threw back her tatty blanket and got out of bed. Maybe Brackenbelly had left, but life at the farm was going to change. Maybe Brackenbelly had helped her uncle to see that he didn't treat her fairly. Maybe she could get a new dress at the market. And some boots.

Isomee walked to her door on her bare feet, but she didn't open it. Hanging on the back of it was a canvas bag and a new halter she had started to make to replace the one she'd given away. Isomee took the bag down, pulled open its drawstring and looked inside. The bolas Brackenbelly had left her as a gift was safely tucked inside. He'd made if from three weights from her mother's old loom, which sat in the barn and gathered dust.

Isomee smiled at the memory of practising with the weapon out on the pasture that she could see outside her bedroom window. As they swung above her head, the three weights had made a high-pitched note that had reminded her of her mother's singing voice.

Isomee had promised herself she would practise with it every day, not so that she could remember Brackenbelly, but so she would remember her mother.

Isomee made sure the bag was closed properly, hung it back up and then went through the door.

On the other side, the kitchen was warm and the logs on the fire were burning nicely.

Uncle Hogg-Bottom was waiting by the front door.

"I've just remembered I've a job I need to do in the barn. Would you mind getting breakfast ready by yourself?"

"No, Uncle," Isomee said, as she crossed to the fire and put the metal grid over the low, flickering flames.

As soon as her uncle was gone, she went into the larder, but, as she had already pointed out to him, it was practically empty. She reached for the bowl of chostri eggs. She'd make an omelette like she had when she'd discovered that Brackenbelly was a vegetarian.

Isomee cracked an egg into a bowl, mixed in some herbs and the last piece of butter they had. Crossing over to the fire, she put the frying pan onto the grid and waited for it to warm up. When it was the right temperature, Isomee poured in the egg mixture and shook the pan around to make sure it spread out evenly. Uncle liked his omelettes thick, level, and above all else, moist, but browned to perfection.

Isomee went to the sink and started to clean up the things she'd already used. The mountains she'd been dreaming about looked back at her through the window. They were there every day — unlike Brackenbelly.

Isomee started to cry as she thought about her friend. He had taught her so much in that one day they had spent together.

The smell of burning wafted up Isomee's nose. With tears blurring her vision, she dashed back to the fire and snatched the handle of the frying pan.

"Ow!"

The handle was red hot. She'd accidentally left it over the flames of the fire and it had heated up. As she pulled her hand away, she caught the edge of the grid with her clenched fist. It shifted and the right-hand edge slipped off the side of the stone ledge of the fire. The frying pan slid down the angled metal and into the burning wood.

Isomee quickly wrapped the material of her skirt around her hand, and pulling the pan out of the fire, put it on the wobbly table.

It was too late.

The food was ruined. Ash and embers covered the top of the now blackened omelette.

Isomee went to the sink and put her hand into the bowl of water that sat at the bottom. She'd burned herself a few times before and she knew exactly what to do. She knew she should have done it sooner, but she had hoped to save the meal. Now that the pain started to go away, fear began to creep up on Isomee.

She'd ruined the food. Uncle would be angry. He'd been in such a good mood for the last day or so, and now she had ruined it.

"If I quickly start again," Isomee said out loud, "I can have another ready before Uncle gets back."

Isomee wrapped her dress around the handle again and then scraped the spoilt food into the bucket where the swill for the pigs was kept. She quickly wiped the frying pan clean, put the grid back above the flames and then went into the larder to get another egg.

It was as she was cracking the egg into the bowl that Isomee realised that something was wrong.

If her uncle was being so nice to her, why was she still so afraid of him?

Three

Brackenbelly's eyes flickered open. It was much later

in the morning than he'd expected. He'd had a busy day the day before and he'd not slept well in the hammock in the barn at Hogg-Bottom farm.

His thoughts instantly turned to Isomee, the girl he'd met there.

Leaving Isomee behind had been one of the hardest things he'd ever had to do. It wasn't as hard as leaving his village and everyone he loved, but it had been close.

The simple truth of the matter was that Isomee couldn't come with him, even if they both wanted it. His life on the road was just too dangerous. Her uncle was a bully, but she was safer with him.

Wasn't she?

Yesterday, Brackenbelly had ridden his new chostri for as long as he could before they both needed to rest and have something to eat. By the end of the day, they'd made it to the edge of a large forest.

Brackenbelly walked into the thick trees and undergrowth for a few yards, found a good place to set up camp, made a meal and a bed and went to sleep.

Bramble, the chostri, settled down just a few feet away.

And now it was time to get up again.

Already.

Brackenbelly got out of bed — a simple mattress of leaves with his cloak as a blanket — and stretched. Bramble was already awake and rummaging through the dead leaves that covered the forest floor, looking for grubs and insects to eat.

"Good morning, Bramble," Brackenbelly said in his deep, gravelly voice. "That looks like a good idea, but my tastes are very different from yours."

He sat cross-legged next to the fire. A human would look at it and see all the usual parts — a slight pit in the ground, a ring of stones to stop the flames from spreading — but there were no ashes and no wood inside it. In the centre of the fire was a fist sized piece of red moss, similar to the golden illumi-moss Brackenbelly had used back at Hogg-Bottom's barn.

Brackenbelly knelt down and started to blow on the moss. He had to get it just right. If he blew too hard it wouldn't work. If he blew too gently it wouldn't work, either. But he'd been using this igni-moss for years and knew how to get it just right. It began to glow, so Brackenbelly stopped blowing and leaned back. He reached forward with his cold hands and put them over the softly glowing moss. It was worth a lot of money and he only used it when there wasn't time to find wood and light a proper fire.

A twig snapped to his right, but Brackenbelly took no notice. He knew it was Bramble. She walked over, moved her head down to look at the moss and then quickly pulled her head back, a look of shock clear on her face.

"Careful, girl. This isn't like the moss you saw me use before. This type generates heat," Brackenbelly said. He stood up and tickled Bramble under her beak. The chostri let out a clucking chuckle and went back to finding something to eat. Bramble was already proving to be good company.

Brackenbelly decided to do the same as the bird. Heading back out to the road by the edge of the forest, he collected some stinging nettles, safe in the knowledge they weren't the ultra-poisonous purple variety. He returned to the fire and detached one of the pockets from his rolled up backpack. He gave it a quick shake and it popped out, turning into a bucket. Using a stick he'd found last night, he hung it over the heat producing moss and popped the nettles inside. Finally, he got a ceramic bottle of water from his pack and added the contents.

"We're going to need more water," Brackenbelly called to Bramble. "I'm not sure we'll find any in this forest unless…"

Brackenbelly got up and let out a sharp whistle. Bramble trotted over towards him, a worm dangling from her beak. She flicked her head back and the worm disappeared inside.

Brackenbelly stepped closer and raised his right hand. Bramble moved her head forward and placed the top of it into Brackenbelly's waiting palm.

Bramble, Brackenbelly thought, *I have tried this before and I think you understood me. Can you talk to me?*

Brackenbelly waited for a reply.

Through the telepathic link, he could feel her curiosity and trust, but nothing else happened. He didn't hear her thoughts inside his own head.

Brackenbelly removed his hand. He could nearly always sense the feelings of animals, but he'd also managed to talk with some by using telepathy.

He was special. Brackenbelly was a Fal-Muru, an uma word that meant The Chosen. They were all

21

blessed with a special gift, or as the uma called it, a Lak-Ti. His gift was the ability to read animals' minds. He had to use this Lak-Ti several times so that he could form a bond — a Chal-Nar — with the animal. Once there was a Chal-Nar, telepathy was much, much more likely.

"We'll try again later," Brackenbelly said and tickled the old chostri under the chin.

When Brackenbelly turned back to the bucket of nettles and water, it was steaming. He grasped the stick and lifted it away from the heat. If the water boiled too much it would all evaporate and then he would be left with nettle sludge and not delicious nettle tea.

Putting the bucket down on a flat rock, Brackenbelly got down on his hands and knees and blew on the moss as hard as he could. The glowing dimmed and when he touched it, the heat had gone.

Brackenbelly packed everything away in his unrolled pack, plucked out the nettles out of the fabric container, and slowly tipped the liquid into his mouth until it was all gone. It was the tiniest bit bitter. He'd undercooked it.

Once the pocket bucket was reattached to the pack, Brackenbelly put his cloak on and slung the pack over his shoulder. He let out another strident whistle and Bramble trotted over, her large, three-clawed feet stomping on the dead leaves and twigs. He placed his hand on her head again and created the Chal-Nar.

Bramble, let's try this again. We need more water. Do you think you could use your sense of smell to find us some? Stamp your foot if you understand me.

Brackenbelly counted to ten and sighed. The Chal-Nar still wasn't completely working.

"Right, girl. Let's explore this forest and see what we can find," Brackenbelly said as he tapped Bramble's knee. She stood on one leg and lifted the joint up. Brackenbelly stepped up onto the handy little step she'd created and swung himself onto her back of soft black feathers.

Clacking his tongue, he gave the bird a gentle squeeze with his legs and they were off, the bird making large, jumping steps across the forest floor.

They made their way through the trees for some time, but didn't find what they were looking for. They stopped for lunch. Once they found their food and ate, Brackenbelly tried the Chal-Nar again. Bramble still didn't seem to understand.

Once everything was packed up and Brackenbelly was happy that he had left no litter and that all was the way he found it, he mounted Bramble.

He had barely squeezed her sides before the chostri was off, moving much faster through the trees than Brackenbelly had expected. Branches whipped past him on both sides, forcing him to duck and sway to avoid them.

"Slow down, girl, there's no rush," he said.

But Bramble took no notice.

She surged forward and Brackenbelly had to grip more tightly with his legs and grasp the reins for fear of falling off. For a moment, he thought that the bird had decided to return to Hogg-Bottom farm, as he had promised she could if she was unhappy, but he soon realised that they were heading the wrong way.

Had she understood the message after all? Had she detected water and was she taking him to it?

Brackenbelly lurched forward on the soft saddle of feathers as the bird suddenly slowed down. Something was wrong. Bramble slowed further and walked over to a large bush of Telaposian holly.

At first, Brackenbelly thought she was still hungry, but then he noticed her footsteps were unusually quiet. Beneath him, Brackenbelly could feel her placing them gently on the ground and shifting them about so as to not tread on anything that would make any noise.

"What is it, girl?" Brackenbelly said, knowing, somehow, that it was not water that the old chostri had found. Bramble shifted and bent her legs, lowering her body to the ground. Brackenbelly swung his leg over her back and dismounted.

A loud bark echoed through the forest.

"Was that a dog?" Brackenbelly said. He moved closer to the holly bush. A growl came from his left. Brackenbelly moved towards it and pulled the branch in front of him further down so he could see.

There were three dogs.

No.

He looked a little closer. They weren't dogs, but jakels — wild dogs that roamed the plains and forests of Kinmara. And these were the worst kind. Holt jakels. Brackenbelly had never seen them before, but he knew about them. They were incredibly fast runners, and worst of all, they had two heads filled with viciously sharp teeth.

The three of them barked and growled at something on the ground at their paws.

Brackenbelly turned back to Bramble and said, "They're just hunting. Come on, let's keep out of their way and move on."

Bramble moved her foot on the ground, snapping a twig.

The growling and barking on the other side of the bush stopped.

Brackenbelly immediately turned his back to the jakels and pulled down the branch.

On the other side, the three wild dogs looked at him through the leaves. One snapped its jaws shut, the second howled. The third drooled.

"I think we've got a problem," said Brackenbelly.

Four

Isomee managed to complete the second omelette

before her uncle came back from the barn. When he saw the remains of the spoilt one in the bin, he didn't say a word.

After the meal, she cleared and washed up, and waited for the next instruction from her uncle.

But none came.

He simply left the table and was off again doing whatever it was that he did when he disappeared. Isomee had never questioned what it was.

Until now.

She sat down at the wobbly table and wondered what he was doing. She really had no idea, so she gave up and tried to think of something to do. Isomee got up and was about to do another of her daily chores when she stopped.

Instead, she went to her bedroom and took the bolas off the back of the door. A wave of guilt washed over her. She had jobs to do and here she was thinking of going out and wasting time with…

Isomee silenced her thoughts. What was she thinking? Even though her uncle was being kind to her, *she* was still acting like his little slave. And it wasn't wasting time, it was having fun. Something else Brackenbelly had taught her.

She stared at the canvas bag in her hands. And decided. She would do it. Uncle was acting strangely, so why not go out and use the bolas. If she was 'wasting time', as he would call it, he would let his guard drop and the real him would appear once more. Then she would know the truth. And perhaps, just perhaps, the new Uncle Hogg-Bottom was the *real* Uncle Hogg-Bottom.

Isomee climbed out the bedroom window and into the bright morning sunshine. She walked across the grass, the blades tickling the soles of her bare feet.

The chostri were out and about, pecking around, looking for things to eat. Thorn, her favourite of all the chostri, trotted over to her.

"Hello," Isomee said. Thorn rubbed his face against hers. It made her smile. "I've made you a new halter to replace the one I gave to Brackenbelly," she said. "I've just got to decorate it. Want to see something brilliant?"

Thorn cocked his head to one side. His large, black eyes glistened as they stared back at her.

Isomee pulled on the draw cord, opened the bag, reached inside and took the ropes. The weights from her mother's loom *clacked* together as they came free from the bag.

The pole that Brackenbelly had set up as a target two days ago was still there. Isomee looked at it, her eyes squinting in concentration, and then began to twirl the bolas above her head. The three pieces of rope snapped tight as the weights whirled round and pulled the ropes taut.

The bolas spun faster above her head.

The holes in the weights began to whistle as the air passed through them. Once she was sure she had enough speed, Isomee let the weapon go. It spun off through the air directly towards the target. It hit the pole and the three stones and ropes wrapped around it.

"Yes!" Isomee cheered and jumped around to face Thorn. He didn't look impressed.

"Suit yourself," Isomee said, and then ran to the pole and began the difficult task of untangling the ropes.

Isomee stayed there all morning and practised. Unlike last time, she wouldn't be late for lunch.

Isomee went back in the house and sat at the wobbly table with the canvas bag. She started to drum her fingers on the table. Should she just make the meal, or should she wait and see what her uncle did?

She continued to wait at the table and soon the hot sun had passed the middle of the sky. Uncle was late. Where on Kinmara was he?

Isomee looked at his bedroom door. They were supposed to be going to the market, too, so where was he? She walked to his bedroom door, raised her hand, and did something she'd never done before — she knocked on it.

There was no answer.

For a brief moment, she thought about going in the room. But that was a step that she wasn't willing to take. Isomee walked away and went in the larder to see what she could turn into a meal.

She was hungry even if he wasn't.

But then she heard the door open behind her.

"Yes," Hogg-Bottom said, his tone short and snappy.

"I'm sorry if I've interrupted you."

"What do you want? I've told you never to disturb me when I'm in my room."

"I'm sorry," Isomee said, looking at the floor. "I was wondering when we're going to the market?"

"We're not going. There's been a change of plan."

"Can we go tomorrow instead?"

"Maybe. I don't know."

He turned to leave.

"Why aren't we going?"

"Because we don't need to," he said over his shoulder.

"Yes, we do," Isomee said looking at the empty shelves in the larder. "We've no food."

"If you want to go on your own…" he said, a smile spreading across his face as he turned back to face her. It was an expression well known to Isomee. It wasn't a pleasant smile.

"You know I can't," she said. "You know I don't know where Kilmiston is."

"No you don't, do you?"

Isomee stepped out of the larder and moved closer to the bolas.

"Why are you being like this again?"

"Oh, Isomee, even when I was being nice to you, I was being nasty."

Isomee eyebrows knitted together. She found herself picking up the bag and hugging it to her chest.

"What do you mean?"

"You're trapped here. You've always been trapped her, which is just the way I like it. I couldn't have you going away with Brackenbelly. What would I do without you?"

Isomee stepped towards her bedroom door.

"You were just being nice to me so that I would stay, weren't you?"

"You're a bright girl, Isomee. Well done."

"I can still go."

"Where?" Hogg-Bottom said, stepping into the kitchen.

Isomee couldn't help it, she flinched and stepped back into her bedroom door, knocking it open and making it crash into the bedroom wall behind it.

"Where will you go, little Isomee?"

"I'll go after Brackenbelly like I should have done yester…" Isomee stopped as the truth of her uncle's cruelty finally dawned on her. "That's why you've been being nice to me. If you could trick me long enough, Brackenbelly would be too far away for me to follow."

Hogg-Bottom slowly clapped his hands together, their sound loud and mocking.

"You're stuck here — forever. And when I die, you'll be all on your own."

Isomee didn't wait to see or hear what Hogg-Bottom did next. She turned and ran through her bedroom, snatched up the new halter she had started making from off her bed, and dived through the window.

Hogg-Bottom's laughter echoed through the house as she flew through the opening and landed on the grass outside. She picked herself up, and the bag with the bolas, and started to run.

The barn didn't usually seem so far away, but today it felt like twice the distance of the racecourse she'd made around the farm. Her eyes darted about, frantically trying to find Thorn, but he was nowhere to he seen. Perhaps he'd gone back into the barn for his usual afternoon nap.

Isomee ran through the open barn doors, the darkness inside taking her by surprise.

"Thorn? Thorn?!" she called, feeling her heartbeat hammering against her chest. She had to get away. This was her only chance or he was right, she would be trapped here forever. Lonely and afraid.

"Thorn," she called again, her voice calmer this time as she searched the dim interior of the building.

From the back of the barn came the rustling of straw. A chostri clicked and cawed.

It was Thorn. She'd recognise the sound of his voice anywhere.

Isomee pulled at the rope that sealed the bolas bag so that it was long enough to be a strap and put it over her head. By the time she'd done it, Thorn appeared out of the gloom and stood in front of her.

"Stay still while I put this on," Isomee said, slipping the halter over his head. "We're going after your mother and Brackenbelly. We can't stay here."

Without being commanded, Thorn raised his knee and Isomee quickly stepped on it and swung onto his back.

"Don't bother going after him," Uncle Hogg-Bottom said from the barn door, making Isomee jump.

He'd followed her. She knew he would, but she'd hoped to be galloping away by the time he made it anywhere near the barn. He was overweight and unfit, but he wasn't even breathing hard. Had it taken her that long to find Thorn and set up his equipment?

"Get out of my way," Isomee said in a voice that sounded much braver than she actually felt.

Uncle Hogg-Bottom sighed. "Poor Isomee, he doesn't want you hanging around with him. He left, and even on Thorn, there's no way you can catch up with him now."

"Thorn's very fast," Isomee said, "especially with my custom made halter."

"You don't know the roads around here. What if he turned off the main road, where would you look? He has a head start of almost two days."

"Chostri have an excellent sense of smell. Thorn will be able to track his mother. If you loved these birds the way I do, you'd know that," Isomee said, feeling her courage and confidence building.

"Be careful with that tongue of yours, child," Hogg-Bottom warned. "Are you really going to leave these birds you say you love so much? Leave the farm? It'll be yours when I die, remember."

"It'll be mine when I'm sixteen."

"It's my farm until I give it to you."

"It's my parents' farm."

"*Was* your parents'," Hogg-Bottom said. "Now, if you've finished being hysterical, get down from there, my lunch needs cooking."

Isomee squeezed Thorn's side with her legs and the chostri brought up his head, made a disapproving snort, and headed for the barn door.

Hogg-Bottom stepped inside the barn and closed the door, sealing them inside, trapping them in almost complete darkness.

"If you get off the bird now, we'll pretend this never happened. This is the only time I will make this offer. If you ride away, there'll be no coming back," Hogg-Bottom said.

Isomee glared into the darkness at where the man had been standing. She knew he could be anywhere now, so she listened carefully, trying to hear his footsteps on the straw bedding that littered the barn floor.

It was impossible to tell. All she could hear was her hammering heartbeat.

Isomee could see the sunlight around the outline of the door. If she could make her way to it, maybe she could charge and burst through the doors. She knew it could only be sealed shut from the outside.

She squeezed Thorn's sides one more time and the chostri moved towards the front of the barn.

"Wait," Hogg-Bottom said from the darkness.

Isomee turned to face the sound, trying to find him. He sounded more desperate than she felt.

"What is it?" she asked, trying to sound confident.

"I have something for you. Your parents wanted you to have it when you were twelve years old. If you leave, I'll burn it and you'll never ever see it."

Isomee felt the blood drain from her pale face.

"You're making it up, just to make me stay. Why have you never told me about this before?"

"Before they left you, I was sworn to secrecy about what they were doing. But I was told if they never came back, I should give something to you when you were twelve — not before."

"Give it to me, now!"

"Don't defy me, child. I'm giving you a chance to say sorry for what you've done, and you throw it in my face. Get down, now! Brackenbelly's gone. He doesn't want you. No one wants you. Not even your mother and father."

Isomee felt a tear roll down her cheek. She was glad they were in the darkness. She didn't want the vile bully to see her cry.

Isomee's heart and mind were in turmoil, but she could only think about one thing — did he really have what he claimed, or was it just a last minute gamble to make her stay?

Five

Brackenbelly looked at the jakels through the bushes.

Perhaps if he showed no fear they would decide he was too big a risk to attack and turn back and carry on with whatever they were doing.

Brackenbelly wasn't that lucky.

The three jakels continued to ignore what had held their attention before and began to walk towards him.

Brackenbelly stepped back and as he let the branch spring back into place, he saw something get up from the ground where the jakels had been looking. It ran away in a flash of black and tan fur.

Was it another jakel?

"I think we'd better get out of here," Brackenbelly said as he dashed back to Bramble.

The faithful chostri lifted her knee up ready, but Brackenbelly had other ideas. He jumped and grabbed a branch above his head, his speed keeping him moving forward. Bringing his knees up, he lifted them up over Bramble's back. Letting go of the branch, Brackenbelly landed on Bramble's soft feathered back.

"Go. Go," he urged the bird.

The chostri started to back up, ready to run, when the first jakel came speeding round the corner of the holly bush.

Now it was closer, Brackenbelly could see that the jakel had three rows of deadly looking teeth. The set at the front looked sharper than the ones behind it, but Brackenbelly had no intention of finding out what any of them were like.

A second jakel came round the other side of the bush.

Where was the third?

"Move. Move!" Brackenbelly said, and kicked Bramble's sides much harder than he intended. The chostri lurched forward just as the first jakel snapped at her legs.

Brackenbelly thought she was going to panic, but the bird stopped, turned her long neck back and looked down behind her. She let out a loud honk at her attacker, picked up her foot and kicked out at the jakel.

Her clawed foot hit the wild dog in the chest, just below its face, and sent the animal rolling backwards across the leaf covered ground.

Brackenbelly twisted around and watched as the jakel stopped itself tumbling by digging its claws into the soft, loamy soil. The second jakel came alongside it. The pair opened their drooling mouths and growled.

"Now you've annoyed them, Bramble. Let's get out of here, before the third arrives." Brackenbelly commanded the old chostri to move with his knees and she moved off, faster than ever before.

As Bramble raced across the forest floor, Brackenbelly looked behind them. Unfortunately, the jakels weren't going to give up. He had no doubt that Bramble could outrun their two pursuers, but the third was still nowhere to be seen. Was it setting up an ambush or had it gone after the thing that had been hidden away on the floor and ran away?

"Bramble, go left, go left," Brackenbelly called, even though he knew she wouldn't understand a word he was saying. He leant over, pulling the reins to the left and squeezed on the left side of her body.

The chostri turned in a slow easy arc. Isomee had trained her well.

Brackenbelly glanced to the left. The jakels were coming, and any distance that Bramble had managed to put between them was being eaten up as they chopped off the corner of the bend that Bramble was taking.

"They're gaining!" Brackenbelly called. He quickly looked over his shoulder. His sword was in his backpack where it was completely useless. He didn't want to hurt the jakels, but if the need arose, they would be in trouble.

Brackenbelly looked ahead, trying to find the clearest route he could, but Bramble seemed to be picking it for herself, swerving from side to side as she ducked between the trees of the forest.

The jakels' barking came louder from behind. They were close and getting closer with every step Bramble took. Brackenbelly needed to think of something clever, and soon, or they would be upon them.

More barking came from ahead.

Was it the third jakel, or had they called in reinforcements?

Brackenbelly remembered how one of them had howled when they had spotted him. Was that a call for help?

Through squinting eyes, Brackenbelly searched ahead, confident he could leave Bramble to decide on the safest route through the trees. His eyes tracked across the floor of the forest searching for wherever the barking came from.

There!

It was a jakel, but it was running away from them. Ahead of it was another with black and tan fur. Was it the animal Brackenbelly had seen flee earlier?

He looked closer, his large uma eyes giving him an advantage in the poor light of the forest. There was something different about the one in front, but they were moving so fast, Brackenbelly couldn't quite work out what it was.

"Bramble, over there," he called and used the reins and his legs to direct the chostri.

Branches flashed past them as they entered a more densely packed area of trees. As one whizzed past, Brackenbelly wasn't quick enough to avoid it. He was slapped across the face.

"G'ah," Brackenbelly cried as he spat leaves out of his mouth.

Bramble looked back over her shoulder.

"Don't look at me, watch where we're going," Brackenbelly called.

Bramble's eyes grew wider for a moment and then she turned her attention to the way ahead.

Brackenbelly looked back and saw what had alarmed the chostri. The jakels had got much closer than he'd expected. Had they stopped barking to conceal how close they were?.

"All right," Brackenbelly said to himself as much as to Bramble. "I think it's time we got out of here."

Brackenbelly leaned to the left and Bramble followed his instruction. They cut across the forest floor.

"Go as fast as you can," Brackenbelly said and nudged his knees into Bramble's side. The chostri started to move faster, the rhythm of her feet speeding up, faster and faster with each stride.

Brackenbelly looked over his shoulder, the two chasers had given up. They were running after their other friend and whoever it was chasing.

"Slow down, girl," Brackenbelly said.

The way the bird's body moved changed and Bramble's speed dropped until soon they were merely trotting along.

Brackenbelly turned Bramble around so they were facing the way they'd come. The sounds of barking died away into the distance. They'd escaped, or, at least, the jakels had decided to pick on an easier target.

And that bothered Brackenbelly.

Bramble swung her neck back and looked at him.

"What is it girl?" he said. Her large, black eyes stared at him. Brackenbelly reached forward and placed his hand on her head to try the Chal-Nar again.

What's bothering you, girl?

There was no response except for the look in Bramble's eyes. Brackenbelly shifted uncomfortably on her back, but it wasn't her feathers that made him feel that way, it was something inside him.

Brackenbelly looked up and searched the area where he had last seen the jakels. There were three against one. He should have helped. If they'd been human or uma he would have.

He closed his eyes and tried to focus on what had been different about the fleeing jakel. It looked different from the others. It was smaller and… Yes, that was it. The jakel only had one head instead of two.

Had they all ganged up on him because he was different? Brackenbelly hung his head. He knew all about being treated badly because he was different.

"I've made a terrible mistake, Bramble," he said. Brackenbelly took his hand off Bramble's head and placed both hands onto the reins. He turned Bramble around.

"I shouldn't have abandoned that jakel. And I shouldn't have abandoned Isomee. Come on, Bramble, we're going back to Hogg-Bottom farm.'

Six

Brackenbelly turned Bramble around and they started

to head back.

If they got a move on, they might make it back to
Hogg-Bottom farm before nightfall. The trees started
to thin out so Brackenbelly nudged Bramble to hurry
up.

The chostri didn't speed up.

"Are you tired, girl? I'm not surprised after all that rushing about," Brackenbelly said, leaning forward and rubbing the top of her head.

The Chal-Nar connected for a moment, even if Brackenbelly hadn't intended it to.

"That's strange," Brackenbelly said, picking up her feelings.

Bramble stepped back.

"You're afraid, girl. What of?" Brackenbelly searched the growing darkness ahead, his large uma eyes taking the dying sunlight from above the canopy of trees and magnifying it.

Brackenbelly swung his leg over Bramble's back and slid down. There was something ahead on the forest floor. He was surprised he hadn't noticed it before, but he had just been in a deadly chase that required all his attention to track the jakels.

"Wait there if you like," he said.

As Brackenbelly moved further ahead, the leaves that covered the ground began to thin out and soon the soft mattress of soil that covered the forest floor was replaced with something much harder.

The trees became sparser and sparser until Brackenbelly stood in a massive clearing. He looked down. There were no trees growing here because there was no soil. None at all. Beneath Brackenbelly's feet was solid rock. But it wasn't all solid. The rock was riddled with holes.

The openings started off quite small, but as Brackenbelly moved further into the clearing, he found that some of them got larger and larger.

He knew that humans called them Dragon Ducts and that they believed that they went deep down into Kinmara's crust. Humans had made plenty of stories designed to explain the mysterious origins of the holes, and for many other things. He also knew that many people, mostly humans, had tried to explore them, but they rarely came back out alive and those that came out would often not talk about their adventures — or misadventures. If he or Bramble fell down one of the larger holes, it would be a disaster. They were well-known for being almost impossible to get out of.

"Let's set up camp for the night," Brackenbelly said to Bramble. "You're tired, and it's getting too dark for you to see. We'll never get back to Isomee before nightfall now, anyway. If we stop now, we can get up early and get there in time for lunch."

Bramble tipped her head to one side. Brackenbelly was sure the chostri looked sad.

"I know, I know," Brackenbelly said to the bird as he took her reins in his hand and started to lead her away from the dangerous holes. He could tell by the tugs and jerks on the strip of leather that she wasn't happy to be moving. It had suddenly got much darker, too.

Brackenbelly stopped and looked around him. Here looked like just a good spot as any other to set up camp for the night.

"Let's take this off," Brackenbelly said, removing the halter.

It had been Thorn's, her son. Isomee had given it to him as a present. It must smell of her child, especially as chostri had such a sensitive sense of smell. Did it not make her miss him?

52

Bramble reached forward with her long neck and stroked her face against Brackenbelly's.

"Go and find something to eat, you deserve it," Brackenbelly said and then started to set up camp.

*

Brackenbelly awoke.

Something was hiding out in the trees — out in the darkness. The fire he had built hours earlier was dying. There was just the gentle glow of bright orange embers left in the bottom of the ring of stones. They would be more than bright enough for someone to spot in the empty darkness of the forest.

He sat up on the pile of leaves he'd collected to act as a mattress and looked out beyond the camp. His cloak was wrapped tightly around him to keep him warm.

Brackenbelly wriggled his arm out and he reached out for his pack. His three fingered hand danced across the floor until he found what he was looking for. He deftly undid his pack as he continued to search for whatever had awoken him. Even with his super-sensitive eyes, he couldn't see anything. Trees and bushes blocked every angle. Perhaps it hadn't been such a good place to camp after all.

Or perhaps whatever was out there was very good at hiding.

Was it the jakels? Had they come back? Had they dealt with the one they were chasing and now they had come back for him? If he knew anything about jakels, it was that they were usually a cowardly bunch. When better to attack Brackenbelly than when he was asleep?

Brackenbelly looked across at Bramble. She was fast asleep on the opposite side of the fire. Her legs were tucked under her body and her long neck has turned back and covered by her wing. She twitched and jerked as if she was in the middle of a dream. Now would not be a good time to wake her.

Brackenbelly picked up a piece of wood from the pile he had gathered before he went to bed and threw it on the fire. A shower of sparks drifted up into the night air. He bent down and blew on the embers, coaxing a bit of life out of them. Flames licked around the edge of the piece of wood, so he added two smaller pieces. Perhaps if whatever were out there knew he was awake, they would give up and go home.

It didn't look like he was going to be that lucky.

A loud screech ripped through the thick darkness. It was a terrible haunting sound and Brackenbelly was amazed that it hadn't woken Bramble. She must be exhausted.

He reached over to his open backpack and snatched up his sword. Whatever was out there had finally decided to come closer.

There came another screech. It was longer and more insistent this time. Still Bramble hadn't woken.

The fire wasn't having the effect Brackenbelly wanted, so there was only one thing left to do. He undid his cloak, swirled it around so that it opened out, and laid it down over the fire.

With the oxygen cut off, the flames were snuffed out and Brackenbelly, like his foe, was safely wrapped in darkness. Now things were even — unless there were three or more jakels.

Another, even louder screech echoed through the trees. It was definitely not a jakel.

Brackenbelly slowly moved his head, using his ears to try and locate the position of the screech more precisely. He stopped. His pointed ears had directed his eyes in the rough area where the sound had come from.

Brackenbelly closed his eyes and listened for a few more moments. When he was satisfied he could hear nothing else out there, he hid the sword behind his back so it wouldn't shine in a stray shaft of moonlight and give him away, and moved off towards his target.

The screech came again, louder, and if he wasn't mistaken, afraid, too.

Brackenbelly stopped. His suspicions were confirmed. He thought he recognised the sound, but now he was sure. It was one he had only recently become familiar with.

He stepped off in the direction of the call when a sharp crack came from his right.

Brackenbelly froze, unsure which way to go. Someone, or something, had stepped on a branch. That meant there were two things out there. How had he missed it?

If the screech was what he thought it was, there was probably nothing to fear, but the branch had been broken by something else and he didn't have a clue to what its identity could be.

Brackenbelly pressed himself against the nearest tree and followed the simple rule: if you stayed still, you were unlikely to be seen. He patiently waited like any skilled hunter and hoped that whatever was out there would run out of patience first and would give itself away again.

He didn't have to wait long.

There was a sudden high-pitched scream, followed by a large splash.

The sound came from no jakel or anything else on four legs. It came from a girl - a human girl.

Wary that it might be a trap, Brackenbelly quietly moved to where the scream had come from. Everything had gone very quiet and his initial suspicions of a trap was replaced with worry. The uma had a feeling he recognised the voice and if it was who he thought it was...

"Brackenbelly," came a quiet voice from the darkness ahead. She sounded afraid, even if she was trying to hide it. "Please say that's you."

The uma stepped forward and saw, now that his eyes had become almost fully accustomed to the darkness, a Dragon Duct.

He leaned forward so he could look over the edge and down into the smooth stone pit that was large enough for a cow to fall into.

"Hello, Isomee," Brackenbelly said, tucking his sword through his belt.

Seven

Isomee wasn't afraid at first — at least the water had given her a soft landing— but as soon as Brackenbelly had identified himself, she took the time to look at her surroundings. It didn't take her long, even hindered by the pale moonlight, to realise there was no way back out of the thing she'd fallen into.

She was inside a smooth rock tube that was almost a perfect circle. There was nothing to hold on to. Nothing at all. It was like being inside a glass bottle or the bowl she used to keep the chostri eggs in - except that had a bottom. Isomee had no idea if this, whatever this was, had one. If there was, she couldn't touch it and she couldn't see it in the light from the moons.

Isomee couldn't believe her luck. Or how clumsy she'd been. After carefully making her way through the forest in case the campfire she'd spotted from the road wasn't Brackenbelly's, she'd snapped a twig, and then in the depth of darkness and panic, fallen into the stone pit she now found herself in.

She was trapped in it, but it was still better than being in the barn with uncle Hogg-Bottom.

Isomee looked up at the star-filled sky. The appearance of her friend's face over the edge of the hole filled her with joy and hope, taking away the cold and fear for a moment.

"Keep kicking. I'll have you out in a moment," Brackenbelly said, his body silhouetted by Kinmara's twin moons.

"Please hurry. There's nothing to hold on to," Isomee replied.

It wasn't just the pit and the cold she was afraid of. All she could think about was what happened in the dream. If Brackenbelly decided she was a burden he might send her back home, and she couldn't go back. Not now.

"You're doing great," Brackenbelly said. "Just keep going."

Afraid to admit it, Isomee looked away from Brackenbelly and said, "I'm not the best swimmer."

She'd learned how to doggy paddle but never to swim properly. Her uncle had taken her to the farm pond one day and pushed her in. She soon found that you could learn to do anything when your life was in danger.

"Well, you're doing great. You can do this, and you'll soon be next to a hot fire," he said calmly.

"Good. This water's freezing," Isomee called with a smile, hoping it would distract him from her fear and clumsiness.

Brackenbelly crouched at the edge of the pit and reached down.

"Just a little further," he grunted.

Isomee carried on kicking at the water beneath her as he stretched and stretched.

It was no good. His arms weren't long enough.

"Let me help," Isomee said.

As soon as she stretched up to meet him, and stopped kicking, she sunk down.

Clamping her lips tight, and squeezing her eyes shut, Isomee panicked as she felt her face slip below the surface. Fear completely overtook her and she thrashed her arms about, raising her terror even higher. She screamed, releasing a stream of bubbles.

And things got worse.

All her air was gone!

She was going to—

Suddenly Isomee remembered to kick her legs. Fuelled by fear, she kicked harder than ever before.

As soon as her pale face broke the surface, she gasped for breath, drawing sweet air in. Her fingers clawed at the smooth rock in front of her but there was nothing for her fingers to grip on to.

"Isomee," Brackenbelly said.

But she didn't hear her friend.

Instead, she carried on kicking, her arms uselessly slapping on the water, throwing it up into her face and sending waves rolling around the inside of the pit.

"Isomee!"

This time, she heard him. Somehow the sound of his voice made her settle back down. Her legs slowly settled back into a rhythm and her arms wafted in the water by her sides as she got her breathing back under control.

"Don't be afraid," he said.

Isomee looked up into Brackenbelly's large eyes. He was worried, she could tell, even if he was trying to hide it. So much for not showing him she was afraid.

"It's going to be all right," he said. "I've got another idea. I'm going to try again. Just concentrate on keeping your head above the water. You'll be out soon — I promise."

Isomee nodded, unable to speak. It was all going to be fine. Brackenbelly would find a way. She trusted him.

The uma laid down on the ground and reached down into the pit towards her with both his arms.

Isomee kicked as hard as she could and felt herself rise out of the water. It was no good. His arms were still out of reach. He was so close, but Brackenbelly might as well have been miles away.

"We need another plan," he said.

"What is this thing I'm in?" Isomee asked.

"It's a…" Brackenbelly said, his words dying away.

"What? What's wrong?"

"Nothing," he said a little too quickly.

"Really?"

"Yes. I just can't remember their names."

Isomee wasn't sure if she believed him about forgetting, but right now she didn't really have a choice. Right now she just needed to get out of the thing, whatever it was.

"Can you keep kicking a bit longer?"

"Yes, but please hurry. This water's freezing!"

"Wait there," Brackenbelly said, stepping away from the edge.

"It's not like I can go anywhere, is it?" Isomee shouted back, hoping a joke would raise her spirits and lighten the mood.

Brackenbelly quickly reappeared over the side and called down, "No, I suppose not."

"Hurry, I'm getting tired," Isomee said, her legs and arms were starting to feel sluggish. The cold was draining her energy.

Was this how it was all going to end? She had defied her uncle and chased after Brackenbelly, only to end up trapped in a great stone pit.

Again she was reminded of the dream she'd had that morning. If only the water was as warm as the water in the beautiful pool she'd landed in.

The silence in the pit made Isomee feel vulnerable. The only sounds she could hear was her fast breathing and the occasional splash of the water as she disturbed it.

Isomee looked down and wondered what was beneath the surface. The water was as black as the night sky above, but Isomee saw the odd flash of her pale feet below her.

Anything could be down there.

Anything.

She quickly pushed the thoughts away. There was no point in frightening herself even more.

From above, came the sounds of movement, but the side of the pit was so high that she couldn't see what Brackenbelly was doing.

Using her hands to steer herself, Isomee moved out into the middle of the pool. As she looked up, a dark blur darted away from the edge of the pit. For a moment, she thought she'd imagined it, but whatever it was scattered a few leaves down towards her.

"Brackenbelly?" she called.

No answer came.

It wasn't Brackenbelly, Isomee realised. The shape had been the wrong colour. But she knew something that was.

"Thorn? Is that you?"

Isomee manoeuvred herself to the far side of the pit, hoping to see more. All she could see was the night sky and the odd branch of a nearby tree. There came more sounds of movement and Isomee wished she could see the ground above.

"Brackenbelly, is that you?" Isomee called.

"Yes, don't worry" came his gravelly voice. "I'm getting a branch to pass down to you. I'm on my way back."

Isomee couldn't remember the last time she'd felt so relieved.

"Is there something wrong?" he called.

"Aside from being trapped down here?" Isomee joked again.

"Yes," Brackenbelly called back to her, clearly not picking up on her true meaning of her words.

"I thought I heard something up there with you," Isomee replied, a slight tremor in her voice.

"Let's worry about you, not me."

"There's something else up there with you, I'm sure."

"Don't worry. I heard it too. There's nothing to worry about. It's your chostri—"

"No. Listen," Isomee said interrupting him. "I thought that, too. But it can't be. I tied Thorn to a tree!"

Isomee heard a vicious snarl and then, out of the corner of her eye, the black blur she'd seen earlier flashed across the top of the pit and dived at Brackenbelly.

Eight

Brackenbelly was pinned down.

He looked up at his attacker. It was a jakel. But it was not one of the small pack that had chased him earlier. This one had only one head. Brackenbelly quickly searched his memory. There were five kinds of jakel on Kinmara, and they all had two heads.

Except for the one he had seen earlier. The one with black and tan fur.

Just like this one.

The jakel's clawed feet pressed down on Brackenbelly's chest, and despite being medium-sized, the wild dog was more than powerful enough to hold him there. It snapped at his face, exposing the three rows of sharp canine teeth.

Brackenbelly's eyes went wide. The jakel's mouth looked more than capable of mauling, maybe even severing, any of his limbs.

Saliva hung from the wicked-looking fangs and flicked and dropped whenever it moved its sleek, pointed head. Its eyes flashed brightly and its large ears were flattened to its head — a clear sign it was angry and filled with hate.

The jakel growled in his face and Brackenbelly brought his arm up. He felt the razor-sharp teeth close around his arm but felt no pain. The hard, leather bracer around his wrist had protected him from harm, if not the dog's foul breath.

"Brackenbelly!" Isomee cried from down the shaft. "What's happening? I can't see you."

"I'm coming," Brackenbelly shouted as he reached behind the jakel's head and grabbed it by the scruff of the neck.

Brackenbelly rolled to the side. As he did so, he pulled on the jakel with all his strength. The canine was thrown clear and hit the ground a few yards away. It yelped in pain as it rolled over and over again, spinning off across the forest floor.

What was he going to do now?

Brackenbelly had to get to Isomee, she was getting colder and more tired by the second, but he had to deal with the jakel first.

Not far away, Brackenbelly spotted a large stick and scrambled over to it. Wrapping his three-fingered hand around it, he held his makeshift weapon out before him, just as the jakel twisted its body and sprung back to its feet.

The wild dog snapped and barked, more cautious of its prey now that Brackenbelly had proved himself a worthy opponent. The jakel moved to the left, keeping its eyes firmly fixed on Brackenbelly, waiting for an opening to attack.

"Brackenbelly! Help!" Isomee cried from the dragon duct. "I don't think I can keep my legs moving much longer."

Brackenbelly quickly glanced at the hole behind him and was about to shout that he was coming when the wild dog attacked. It ran straight at him, jumping at his chest, its paws out ready to knock him off his feet and down into the hole.

Brackenbelly dived to the right.

The jakel flew through the air and landed in the spot where Brackenbelly had been moments before. It skidded on the ground and then pitched forward, going head-over-heels. Its rear end went over the edge of the pit and its feet desperately scratched at the ground, trying to stop itself falling in. But the jakel's claws couldn't get a grip on the thin layer of mud that covered the rocky rim. As the last of the soil came away from beneath the jakel's scratching feet, the dog slipped over the edge and toppled into the shaft.

"No! Brackenbelly shouted.

It might have attacked him, but Brackenbelly couldn't let the creature get trapped, or land on Isomee.

Brackenbelly ran to the edge of the hole and threw himself to the ground. He slid over the edge and into the dragon duct, close behind the panicking dog.

At the last moment, his left hand caught the lip of the hole, his three strong fingers gripping onto the rounded edge, while his other hand made a grab for the jakel's foot.

And missed.

Brackenbelly watched helplessly as his worst fear came true. Isomee let out a short scream as the jakel crashed into her. The terrified sound was suddenly cut off as Isomee and the jakel disappeared below the surface of the black water.

Brackenbelly hung above the sloshing water, his fingers going white with the strain, and watched. The water slowly settled back to its normal, flat state, but neither Isomee nor the jakel reappeared. Only the reflection of Kinmara's twin moons stared back at him, reminding Brackenbelly of Isomee's frightened eyes. He grasped the lip of the pit with both hands and pulled himself up.

Isomee must have been in the water for two or three minutes already, and under it for at least another ten seconds.

He had to get to her, and fast.

There was only one problem. If he got in the hole, he'd never get out.

Brackenbelly scrambled to his feet and looked around for something to use. He spotted some vines hanging from a tree. Drawing his sword, he ran over to it and swiftly sliced through one of the vines. Dropping his weapon, he grabbed the severed end and charged at the edge of the dragon duct. He dived in, the vine trailing behind him.

The freezing water almost took his breath away as he shot through it like a spear. As soon as he began to slow down, Brackenbelly began to swim, dragging the vine behind him. He kicked his legs furiously and used his arms to push his way down deeper, penetrating into the darkness of the water.

He wasn't sure how long he'd been swimming, but his lungs began to ache and he knew that if he didn't find the girl soon, he would have to resurface, take in some more air and try again.

But that would mean that Isomee would be under for even longer. Brackenbelly had no choice but to push onward until he could take no more.

Just as he thought he couldn't hold his breath any longer and would be forced to give up, he saw something off to the right.

An object glimmered weakly in a beam of bright moonlight as it pierced the gloom for a moment.

It was her.

It was Isomee.

Brackenbelly recognised her tattered dress, not to mention her red hair. The moonlight had caught on a silver necklace as her body twisted in the water.

Letting go of the vine, Brackenbelly reached out, grasped her wrist and pulled Isomee towards him. He kicked and made for the surface knowing he had little time left. Isomee would have even less.

The moons grew larger and less distorted above him and he could tell he was getting nearer to the surface. Brackenbelly broke through, Isomee clamped tight to his side and filled his lungs with a deep gulp of air. He swam with her to the edge of the duct and grabbed the vine, which dangled down the inside.

Isomee coughed and Bracekneblley couldn't help but smile. If she could cough she was breathing, and if she was breathing she was alive.

All he had to do was get her out and warm her up — and fast.

Brackenbelly shifted the girl onto his back, reached up as far he could, grabbed the vine and started to pull.

He was just about to grab the edge when something grabbed his foot and dragged him back down into the water.

Nine

Brackenbelly crashed back down into the dragon

duct, let go of Isomee and disappeared beneath the

surface.

He looked down at what had his foot as he slipped
further down into the cold, dark water. What he saw
wasn't a surprise.

It was the jakel.

The wild dog's mouth was firmly clamped around
his boot.

Brackenbelly looked up through the churning water above and saw Isomee floating on the surface. He had to get back to her, but he didn't want to hurt the jakel either. Uma were taught to respect life and live in harmony with nature. He had to try and save the poor thing — if it would let him.

He reached down, placed his hand on the top of the wild dog's head and looked into its eyes.

Let go, he said into the jakel's mind.

Nothing happened. It carried on biting, dragging them both down. Brackenbelly hadn't expected it to work but it was worth a try.

Then he had another idea.

He reached out with his other hand and placed it on top of the one that was already on the jakel's head.

I remember you. Do you remember me? I wanted to help you, but I thought you had escaped the others. Swim to the surface and I'll help you now.

Brackenbelly looked down, a trail of air bubbles escaping from his mouth.

The jakel still hadn't let go. Was it trying to kill him, or just holding on in fear?

Why does my Lak-Ti never *work when I need it t—*
?

Before he'd finished thinking the question, the jakel let go of his foot. And not a second too soon. His lungs were ready to burst.

Brackenbelly made huge sweeps with his arms and powered to the surface. He needed to get back to the vine and get them all out — now.

But something wasn't right.

Brackenbelly could feel it.

He looked down.

The jakel wasn't swimming up and following him, it was sinking down.

Brackenbelly stopped for a moment and looked up at Isomee. He had to get to her, he had to get to the surface for himself too, but he wanted to save the jakel too.

He looked at the wild dog through the dark water and Brackenbelly realised why it wasn't moving. The decision had been made for him. It was already too late to save the dog.

Brackenbelly kicked for the surface.

Isomee was right above him as he broke the surface. He pulled her tight to him and swam toward the edge of the smooth cylinder. Her face was blue and her eyes were closed. She wasn't moving.

"Isomee," Brackenbelly said to her. She didn't answer. He shouted her name and shook her as his short legs tried to keep them afloat.

She still didn't answer.

Brackenbelly began to feel his hopes dwindle. He was too late and he'd lost them both.

Then he felt something hot on his cheek. It was Isomee's breath. It was very weak, but she was alive.

Now all he had to do was get her out of the cold water before it was too late.

Shifting Isomee onto his back, he swam to the vine and grabbed it in one hand. He wrapped the end around both Isomee and himself and then tied it off. Once he was sure she was securely fixed to his back, he placed his feet against the rock face and braced himself for the climb.

The shaft would normally have been an easy task for the strong, muscled uma to climb, even with the girl on his back, but the freezing water and the fight with the jakel had sapped his strength. Not to mention he should have been fast asleep right now.

Teeth gritted, Brackenbelly gripped the edge of the dragon duct and half climbed, half rolled out, careful not to injure Isomee as he did so.

Picking up his sword, Brackenbelly cut the vine from the tree, leaving Isomee strapped to his back. He crouched down and moved the girl into a piggyback position.

They must have made a lot of noise because Bramble awoke as they came crashing through the undergrowth. She strutted towards them, clearly happy to see both her new and old masters.

"We need to warm Isomee up, quickly," Brackenbelly said to the giant bird as he placed the girl beside the fire.

He pulled the cloak off the top of the fire and the sudden gust of air made the embers glow warm and red. It was nowhere near hot enough to warm Isomee up, though. Brackenbelly wrapped the blanket around her and threw more wood onto the fire.

"Bramble," he called to the bird. "Please let this work," he muttered under his breath as he placed his hand on her head and said, "Use your wings to send a blast of air at the embers and heat up the fire."

Bramble began to lift her legs up and down as if she were marching. At the same time, she raised and lowered her wings. The gust of air they produced made the flames brighter and hotter and the wood that Brackenbelly put onto the fire was soon starting to smoke and smoulder.

"Good girl," he said. "Don't stop. Let's just hope we're not too late."

Ten

Isomee awoke.

"It wasn't a dream," she said as she pulled herself upright and hugged Brackenbelly's cloak closer to her. The heat from the fire had made it cosy and warm, but now the flames were all but gone. Her dress was dry and covered in creases from where she'd slept in it.

On the other side of the fire, Brackenbelly was fast asleep. So was Bramble.

Isomee stared at the bird for a moment, pleased to see her once again, and then out into the forest. Throwing the cloak to one side, she quietly climbed out of bed and wandered off into the forest, carefully placing her naked feet.

Everything looked different in daylight, but Isomee was sure she could find what she was looking for.

Finding the pit she had fallen into was easy. Brackenbelly had left an obvious track through the trees. His footprints looked very deep in the soft soil.

He must have carried me back, she thought.

Around the edge of the pit, there were signs of a struggle.

Isomee remembered how Brackenbelly had been attacked. All she could hear from inside the hole were the animal's growls. Then it had fallen down on her.

That was as far as her memory went.

She carried on walking through the forest. What seemed to take her a lifetime in the dark only took a few minutes to walk in the daylight.

The silence of the forest was broken by a click and a caw off to her left.

"Thorn!" Isomee cried, dashing to his side. He was sat at the base of the tree she'd tied him to last night. "I'm sorry I left you here. I didn't mean to be gone so long."

Thorn pushed himself against her and rubbed his face against hers. He was obviously pleased to see her again, despite being abandoned.

"I've found your mum and Brackenbelly," Isomee said. "I know they'll be pleased to see you. It's not far. Come on."

Isomee untied Thorn from the tree and walked back to the campsite. On the way she stopped and picked up some fresh wood to use as fuel.

Bramble and Brackenbelly were still fast asleep when she wandered back into the clearing. Thorn walked over to his mother whilst Isomee put the wood she had collected onto the fire. She blew on it to bring the flames back up.

Bramble stirred from her sleep and leapt to her feet in surprise and excitement.

Isomee smiled as she watched mother and son groom each other. It was wonderful to see them happy to be in each other's company once again.

The fire popped, and Isomee wasn't sure if it was that, or the contented noise the chostri were making, that woke Brackenbelly up. He sat up and gave a big yawn. He had dribble running down his chin.

"Sorry to wake you," Isomee said as she threw some more wood onto the fire.

"It's fine. We need to get moving anyway," Brackenbelly said as he sat up, leaned towards the fire and rubbed his hands before the rising flames.

Isomee looked at Brackenbelly and smiled. "Thank you for saving my life," she said.

"You're welcome. Just don't make a habit of it. That's twice now," Brackenbelly said without a trace of humour in his voice. "How did you find me?"

"I was going to stay at the farm, really," Isomee said. "Uncle had changed, or so I'd thought, but then he showed his true colours again. I decided to come after you even though you had a massive head start.

Uncle was only being nice to me because he thought I wouldn't dare follow you."

"So why did you?"

"As I said, he showed his true colours," Isomee stopped and felt sad for a moment. She really had thought he'd changed. "Then he trapped me in the barn and tried to bully me into staying. But even his promises weren't enough to make me stay. They were probably lies, anyway."

Isomee looked across at Brackenbelly. He was sat looking at her with an expression that suggested he wanted to say something but didn't know what.

"Anyway," Isomee continued, "I climbed up into the hayloft, waited for him to follow me up there and then climbed out the external doors using the winch. I knew he'd be too scared to follow me out there. He shouted at me as I ran away, but by the time he guessed what I was up to, it was too late."

"And what were you up to?" Brackenbelly asked.

"I ran back round to the barn's main doors, threw them open, grabbed Thorn and rode away."

Brackenbelly got up and walked over to the two chostri. He gave them a friendly stroke on the beak and then returned to the warmth of the fire.

Isomee poked the fire and said, "How come you're so close to the farm? To be honest, I was never thought I'd see you again. I saw a fire through the trees as Thorn and I came up the road, but I didn't expect it to be you."

"I saw something that made me realise I'd made a terrible mistake. I shouldn't have left you behind, Isomee. I'm sorry."

"Don't be. I understand why you left," she said, remembering her dream. "So, where are we heading?"

"It's a dangerous life I lead, as you found out last night. Coming with me may not be the best idea."

"I know," Isomee said, thinking about her dream as well as her time in the pit. "As much as I love my farm and the animals on it… I'm not meant to be a farmer. I'm…"

"What?" Brackenbelly said.

"My uncle would say I was wrong. Nothing but a foolish girl."

"Your uncle isn't here."

Isomee smiled and decided to tell him what she was going to say.

"I want to see the whole of Kinmara."

"Why do I suspect it's more than that," Brackenbelly said with a smile.

"I'm meant to do something special with my life, I can feel it. Maybe I'm meant to be — what was it you called yourself? — a Fal-Muru."

"I'm not sure humans can be," Brackenbelly said and got up again. "Wait here, and don't move," he ordered and then picked up his pack and wandered off into the woods.

Isomee watched him go. Was it just her, or had Brackenbelly changed the subject very quickly?

Brackenbelly returned a few minutes later with a couple of branches in his hand and a bucket.

"Where did that come from? And what's in it?" she asked, pointing at the bucket.

Then she noticed it was made from the same fabric as his pack and that one of the pouches was missing from its side.

"No wait, I've guessed."

"You're very observant, Isomee. Except for when there's an enormous hole in the ground in front of you."

"It was dark!" Isomee protested with a laugh.

Brackenbelly put the two sticks together — one had a Y shape at the top — and used it to hang the fabric container over the flames.

"Won't that burn?" Isomee asked, pointing at the bucket.

"No. Watch. The uma are clever inventors. We've learned to take what nature has given us and use it to make our lives easier, without damaging our environment," he said. "This pocket bucket is made from a natural fibre that we've discovered. It's strong and heat resistant. My cloak is made from the same material. Look."

Isomee turned and saw that the water inside the bucket was already boiling.

"Fancy a cup of tea?" Brackenbelly asked.

"Yes, please. What kind?'

"Nettle."

"Nettle?"

"Yes, nettle."

Isomee looked at Brackenbelly doubtfully.

"It sounds disgusting."

"Have you ever tried it?"

"No."

"Then how do you know?"

"Well…"

"I thought you wanted to explore Kinmara?" Brackenbelly said.

"I do."

"If you're going to live on the road with me, you'll have to get used to sleeping in all sorts of different places and eating whatever's available. Travelling and exploring doesn't sound so glamorous now, does it?"

Isomee stood up straight. She wasn't going to let him think she would be put off so easily.

"Very well. I'll try it, and you can tell me more about the Fal-Muru."

"What do you want to know?" he asked, stirring the nettle tea.

"If humans could become one, what do I need to do?" Isomee said, smiling.

"If you knew, you wouldn't be smiling."

"Why? What's so terrible?"

Brackenbelly was quiet for a while and then said, "You have to die."

Eleven

"You have to die?" Isomee asked, shocked at Brackenbelly's answer.

"That might have been a slight exaggeration," Brackenbelly said, as he took two smaller pockets off the side of his pack.

Isomee watched as he shaped them into cylinders that fitted nicely into his hand.

Brackenbelly balanced them on top of the ring of stones that encircled the fire and then, lifting the bucket off the stick frame, poured the nettle tea into them.

"Here," he said, handing one over. "The gift is given to you when you least expect it — when you don't want it, but you *need* it."

"I don't understand," Isomee said as she blew over the top of her drink to try and cool it down.

"Well, for example, I was attacked by a cat."

"A cat?" Isomee said. She sipped at her tea and looked up at Brackenbelly. "This tastes… interesting."

"Keep drinking, you'll grow to love it, I promise."

"I'm not sure I believe you," she said with a playful smile. "But your gift, you said you had to die, or almost die, or something. How could a cat almost kill you?"

Brackenbelly put his cup down on the fireplace and looked over at the two chostri. They had gone off into the woods to find their breakfast.

He was uncomfortable talking about it, Isomee could tell. Perhaps she shouldn't have asked him about it.

Brackenbelly picked the cup back up, took a sip and continued.

"It was no house pet that attacked me. It was a puma cub. I was only seven or eight and I found it all alone in the woods by our village. I picked it up so I could play with it and it stuck its claws into my stomach. It's why I'm called Brackenbelly."

Isomee scrunched up her eyebrows while Brackenbelly got to his feet. He pulled aside his tunic.

"What's that?" Isomee said.

On his belly, his skin was pinched and misshapen. It made a shape that looked a little bit like a bracken leaf.

"It's a scar."

"What's one of those?" Isomee said, shaking her head.

"May I?" Brackenbelly asked as he reached out for her hand.

Isomee nodded.

"What's that, there?" he asked, pointing to a mark on the end of her finger.

Isomee went quiet and tried not to remember the day it happened. She had prepared dinner, but uncle had decided that the vegetables weren't cut small enough. He made her do it again and she had accidentally cut her finger because she couldn't see properly through her tears.

"You cut yourself, yes?" Brackenbelly asked.

Isomee nodded, unable to say anything.

"That's a scar. It's when we damage our skin and it re-heals itself. I got this from the puma as it sunk its claws into me. I remember it hurt — a lot. I was told many years later I was lucky to be alive."

"But how does that give you the power? Does everyone have the same one? What other powers have you seen? I'd love to be able to read people's minds."

"Slow down. That's a lot of questions," laughed Brackenbelly. "I've never read people's minds, only animals. And it's not as simple as that. It takes time, trust and practice to be able to do it."

"So," Isomee started, unsure whether to ask, "how did you get it? The power, I mean."

"The puma had its claws inside me and as it held on, I grabbed its head in my hands and shouted for it to let me go. Then it happened. I was given the Lak-Ti."

"Lak-Ti?"

"It's what we call the gift in my language," Brackenbelly explained.

"Fal-Muru. Lak-Ti. I like your language. So," Isomee said, returning to the puma story, "did it let go?"

"Oh yes! Being granted a Lak-Ti is very painful, both physically and mentally," Brackenbelly paused for a moment. "In that instant, I was given telepathy and it caused a telepathic link between us straight away. The pain I was feeling was passed to the puma as well, so it let go."

"But why were you given a — what was it, a Lak-Ti — then?" Isomee asked.

Brackenbelly nodded, showing her she had said it right, and said, "They say that if you are one of the Fal-Muru, the Lak-Ti is given to you in a moment of pain, of dire need, when your life depends on it. It's like the feeling and fear somehow unlocks your special ability."

Isomee thought about what the uma was saying. It meant that the puma cub must have almost killed Brackenbelly when it attacked him.

"I think I've changed my mind. I don't want a Lak-Ti."

"If it's meant to be, Isomee, it's meant to be, and you can't escape," Brackenbelly said. "I know one thing that's meant to be, though."

"What's that?" Isomee asked, curious to know what he was thinking.

"You need some boots and clothes that are more appropriate for adventuring."

Isomee looked down at her tatty grey dress and nodded.

"I've come in everything I own."

"It doesn't matter. You don't want to own too many things when you're on the road," Brackenbelly said and lifted up his pack. "Mind you, now I have Bramble, I might be able to carry a few more things."

"So, where are we going?" Isomee said, returning to her original question.

"I think we'd better head for the nearest town and get the things we need."

"Where's that?"

"If we carry on through the forest we'll find a village called Bently. It's quite small, but they should have everything we need."

"How long will it take us to get there?"

"Depending on how fast we push the chostri. At least a couple of days."

"Is there nowhere closer?"

"No. Why?"

"Can we get something to eat before we start?"

"Are you hungry?"

"Starving," Isomee admitted.

Brackenbelly looked over his shoulder at the chostri.

"I'm sorry. We uma don't need to eat as much as humans do. It looks like Bramble and Thorn have found a nice nest of grubs to eat, but I expect you'd like something more… appetising."

Isomee looked over at the two chostri. They appeared to be working as a team to lure the grubs out of their underground home.

"Are you going to eat?" she asked.

"If you are."

"I'll have whatever you're having."

Brackenbelly held out his hand so he could pull her up to her feet.

"Let's see what nature has given us."

*

Isomee finished off the nuts and berries they'd found in the nearby forest, while Brackenbelly cleaned up the campsite.

It had been fun finding them, but Brackenbelly had warned her never to go looking on her own. Berries, in particular, could be very poisonous if you didn't know what you were looking for.

"We need to make sure this is out, too. We don't want to be responsible for any forest fires," he said, stamping on the last few remaining embers. "Are you ready to move on?"

"Yes," Isomee said, stuffing the last few berries into her mouth. Once it was clear again, she shouted, "Thorn!"

The chostri skipped up beside her and Isomee quickly mounted him.

Brackenbelly and Bramble trotted up beside them.

"Ready?" he asked.

"Yes. Are you?" Isomee answered, looking at his face. "You look a bit nervous."

"We ran into some trouble yesterday, but I'm sure it's nothing we can't steer around if we need to, and I know you're an excellent rider."

"After you," Isomee said.

Brackenbelly clacked his tongue and Bramble moved forward.

"Keep your eye out for those pits," he warned.

"You never did tell me what they were called."

"No, I didn't," Brackenbelly answered and sped off on Bramble, sending up a shower of dried leaves as her clawed feet gripped the ground.

Isomee sat and watched for a while as the large bird and her rider went off through the trees.

He was acting strange.

"Why won't you tell me what they're called?" she shouted, but Brackenbelly still didn't answer. "Come on, Thorn," Isomee said, and with a squeeze of her legs, they were off.

Isomee and Brackenbelly rode through the forest, the bright sunshine above came and went as they passed through thicker parts of the forest as well as wide clearings.

They rode for hours with only the odd bit of conversation. Eventually, her stomach started to growl again.

"Are we going to stop to eat soon?"

"Again?"

"I'm sorry," Isomee said, suddenly feeling very awkward.

"It's all right. Let's keep going until we find something suitable."

"That sounds fair," Isomee said.

Bramble let out a cry of pain, shattering the silence of the forest. Brackenbelly was thrown from her back as she fell to the ground.

"Are you all right?" Isomee said, pulling on Thorn's reins and starting to dismount so she could help him.

"Don't move!" Brackenbelly shouted as he got back to his feet. "Any of you."

Twelve

"What's wrong?" Isomee asked, her head turning quickly, looking for any sign of danger through the trees.

"Look down," Brackenbelly said, getting up off the floor.

Isomee did as Brackenbelly suggested. At first, all she saw were twigs, leaves and small, green plants. Then she looked past them at what was beneath and took in a sharp breath

"I see them," Isomee said, "They look like smaller versions of that pit I fell in. Much smaller."

Brackenbelly nodded.

"Dragon ducts. Just the right size for a chostri to step in and lose her footing. Are you all right, Bramble?"

The chostri clambered back to her feet. Isomee watched as the great bird looked around for a safe place to put her feet. She didn't need Brackenbelly's Lak-Ti to tell the bird was nervous.

"We must be careful," Brackenbelly said.

"Hang on a minute," Isomee cried. "Did you say dragons? Here? There's no such thing as dragons. If they were real I would have seen them flying through the air."

"I'm well aware of that," Brackenbelly said. "It's just what humans call these holes."

"What do uma call them?"

Brackenbelly appeared to think about for a moment and said, "Annoying."

Isomee laughed even though she thought Brackenbelly probably wasn't joking.

"Very funny. Is that why you didn't tell me what they were called?" she asked. "Did you think I'd be afraid?"

"Yes," Brackenbelly answered as he crouched down and inspected Bramble's leg.

Isomee wanted to get down and help, but Brackenbelly had told her not to move and she was going to do what she was told. She looked at the chostri from where she was sitting. Bramble's foot seemed uninjured, at least there were no cuts that she could see.

"Is she unharmed?" Isomee asked.

"She's fine," he said. "It was probably the shock that made her cry out."

"That's a relief. So is it safe to move on?"

"Let's give it a few minutes so she can rest it."

"It's better to be safe, I suppose. So, dragons. I don't believe in them. They're just stories. Dad used to tell—" Isomee stopped.

Brackenbelly smiled at her. She wanted to finish the sentence, but she couldn't. Thinking about her parents was too painful.

"Stories are important, even if they aren't true," he said, breaking the silence.

"Then why are they called dragon ducts if there're no such things as dragons?"

"Climb down and I'll tell you. We'd better walk through this part of the forest. And keep a close eye out. These ducts are everywhere. We can't afford for Bramble or Thorn to break a leg. Or us for that matter."

Isomee swung one leg over Thorn's back and slid off.

"Now, be careful," Brackenbelly warned. "Some of the ducts have been covered by dead vegetation and are difficult to see."

Isomee nodded and they began to lead Bramble and Thorn by their reins.

The four of them moved forward in silence, all their attention fixed on looking for danger. Isomee's eyes darted left and right searching for the dreadful little holes, but soon she settled into a routine of looking ahead and sweeping her eyes from side to side as she learned what signs to look for.

They walked in silence for what felt like an age until Isomee could bear it no more. She had so much she wanted to learn.

"You were going to tell me about dragon ducts," she reminded Brackenbelly.

"Yes, I was," he answered. "It is said that once, before man ruled the land, mighty dragons shared it with them, just as the jakel, the chostri and the uma do now."

"How long ago?" Isomee asked.

"I don't know," Brackenbelly answered. "There were dragons of all shapes and sizes, and not all of them were evil, though most people today - humans anyway - think they were. In fact, hardly any were. It is thought that they only attacked people because humans began to grow in number and were taking over their land to turn into farms and villages."

"So where did they all go?" Isomee asked.

It was an interesting story.

Even if she didn't believe it.

"It's said that a long time ago there was a great disaster. No one really knows for sure what it was, but some of the ancient elders believe that many fire mountains all across Kinmara, or perhaps one super fire mountain, erupted and blocked out the sunlight and sent Kinmara into an ice age."

"Ice age? Are you saying that everything got so cold, because there was no heat from the sun, that everything turned to ice?" Isomee asked.

"Well, I'm not sure about everything, but yes. Anyway, other elders and Wise Ones think an enormous rock came from the heavens and crashed into Kinmara throwing millions and millions of tonnes of dirt and soil into the air, also blocking out the sun's warm rays. Others think the world got too hot and the icecaps at the top and the bottom of Kinmara melted, the seas rose and there was a great flood."

"Top and bottom?"

"Yes, Kinmara is a sphere, a ball, just like its moons, remember?"

"Yes, I remember. You've told me before, the day we raced at my farm. My uncle always told me the world was flat."

"I don't think your uncle was trying to trick you. Not this time, anyway. Most humans think it is."

"So," Isomee said, wanting to bring the conversation back to the dragons. "How would those disasters get rid of the dragons?"

"Whatever it was that blocked out the sun, or made the seas rise, the story goes that the dragons all teamed up for their own survival and left the humans behind to their own fate. The fire-breathing dragons used their breath to burn holes deep into the land—"

"Is that why they're so smooth?" Isomee interrupted.

"What? The dragons?" Brackenbelly said.

Isomee looked up into his smiling face.

"You know what I mean. The ducts, silly."

"That would make sense," Brackenbelly answered. "The heat would melt the rock. Anyway, the dragons disappeared below the ground and some people say that they're still waiting down there, deep in the middle of Kinmara, waiting to one day return and reclaim the world as their own."

"I don't believe it," Isomee declared, shaking her head.

"Why not?"

"Well, what about all these small holes?" Isomee asked as she pointed at the ground. "Are you telling me there were dragons that small?"

"Maybe there were," Brackenbelly answered, "but some people think that they were vents to let out all the smoke and gases created by the melting process of the rock."

Isome thought for a moment.

"That still doesn't make sense. When the dragons burned their way down through the ground, where did the melted rock go?"

Brackenbelly was quiet for a moment.

"And, why didn't it hurt them?"

"Hmmmm," said Brackenbelly.

"Have I finally found a question you can't answer?" Isomee teased.

When Brackenbelly didn't respond she turned and looked at him. He was holding his breath and his head was tipped slightly as if he was listening carefully.

"Get on Thorn, quickly," Brackenbelly said in a hushed voice.

"Why?"

"We have company. Bad company."

Thirteen

Isomee took hold of Thorn and leapt onto his back in one easy movement.

"Quick, back the way we came," Brackenbelly shouted as he picked up the reins, kicked Bramble into action and turned her around.

"You said we shouldn't ride through here, that we could hurt them," Isomee protested.

"I know, but we need to get away from here — from them!"

Isomee turned and looked over her shoulder. At first, there was nothing, but then sounds of barking echoed through the forest.

"What is it we're running from?"

"Some old friends."

Isomee peered closer at the approaching shapes. At last, she could make out what they were.

"They're just dogs."

"No, they're not. They're holt jakels. I've already run into them once. Trust me, we don't want to mess with them. Go! Go!" Brackenbelly shouted.

Isomee squeezed Thorn's sides and the chostri surged forward. She clamped her legs hard, gripped the reins, and crouched as low as she could.

She quickly looked behind her. Brackenbelly was kicking Bramble and the old chostri chased after her son, keeping up despite her age.

Below her, Isomee could feel Thorn's long legs half step, half jump as he looked down at the ground and skilfully placed his fast moving feet between the holes.

Isomee and Thorn raced ahead, her skill as a chostri rider giving her a clear advantage over her friend. She slowed back down. Brackenbelly would probably be happy that she was further ahead, but she didn't want to leave her friend behind.

She saw Brackenbelly glance over his shoulder. Curious about what he'd seen, she looked too. Isomee's eyes widened. The jakels were gaining ground. She was beginning to see what Brackenbelly meant. The jakels were going to be dangerous. Not only were they fast, they also had two heads. Inside their mouths were several rows of gnashing, snarling teeth.

Isomee quickly counted her pursuers.

Five.

Five very angry, vicious, two-headed wild dogs were getting closer by the second.

"What do we do?" Isomee screamed back at her friend.

"We keep riding. If anything happens to me, just keep going. Understand?"

"No way!" Isomee shouted and glanced over at Brackenbelly. He had drawn his sword and was riding one handed.

Isomee reached behind her. The bag with the bolas was strapped to Thorn's back. If she could get to it…

She reached behind her but it was no good. As fast as he was going, Thorn was moving about too much for her to feel the knot that fastened the drawstring. There was no way she was going to be able to untie it while they were still moving.

"All right, I've another idea," Isomee said. "Thorn, we've done this a hundred times before."

Without another word, Isomee swung her leg over Thorn's back and dropped to the ground as it flew past at break-neck speed.

Brackenbelly tightened his grip on Bramble's sides with his thighs. The jakels were getting closer by the second and it was unlikely that Bramble could go much faster with all the dangerous dragon ducts littering the place.

He would have to try and slow the jakels down instead.

Behind him a jakel charged forward, both heads snapping and snarling. He brought the sword across his body ready for a backhand swing.

It wasn't the most powerful attack he could use, but he hoped it would be able to do what he needed. He didn't want to hurt the jakels, he only wanted to frighten them off.

Brackenbelly waited for the right moment to put his plan into action as tree after tree rushed past him on either side. He needed the right tree and the right time.

Now!

He brought the sword up with as much power as his muscles could manage.

Brackenbelly's uma blade was strong, flexible and sharp. It sliced cleanly through the branch he'd aimed at. He ducked as it fell behind him and carried on riding.

A few steps of Bramble's thundering feet later, he glanced back to see if he'd been successful.

The branch crashed to the floor, catching the two-headed dog off guard. It panicked for a moment but jumped at the last minute. For a split second,

Brackenbelly thought that his efforts had failed and his pursuer would escape his trap, but the branch tumbled and skidded across the half stone, half mud floor. At the last moment, a smaller, side branch flicked up and slapped the jakel on the end of one of its black, wet noses.

The animal's whimper filled the forest for a moment but Brackenbelly turned his attention back to where he was going. He searched ahead, looking for Isomee and Thorn. They were just ahead of him, but they were in trouble. Brackenbelly's stomach filled with dread.

Isomee was falling off.

Isomee wasn't falling. She knew exactly what she was doing.

She slid down Thorn's smooth feathers and her feet hit the floor. With practised skill, she bent her knees to soften the impact. The energy of the moving ground catapulted her back into the air. She twisted her body and landed on Thorn's back again — only now she was facing backwards.

"Well done, Thorn," she said, patting the chostri's feathers.

She quickly checked on Brackenbelly. His mouth was wide open for a moment, and then it turned into a smile. She must have impressed him.

Isomee turned her attention to the canvas bag. It was much easier to get inside now she was facing the right way. As soon as the knot was untied and the bag was open, she sent her hand inside and pulled out the bolas.

Now all she had to do was repeat the drop and spin trick so she was facing the right way.

*

Brackenbelly had to admit he was impressed. Isomee was clearly a skilled rider. He would need to get her to teach him that trick, and anything else she could get the chostri to do.

He heard barking. Three jakels were still in hot pursuit.

"Come on, girl," he urged Bramble.

The jakels were getting closer and the old bird was getting tired.

A jakel, racing as fast as its legs could carry it, pulled up alongside the chostri. Brackenbelly pulled on the reins and Bramble, following the command, swerved to the left.

Brackenbelly drew his sword and stabbed toward the chasing dog, which leapt out of the way and snarled at its attacker.

Another jakel came from the left. Brackenbelly let go of the reins for a moment and put the sword in his left hand.

Without warning, Bramble suddenly swerved around a patch of poisonous purple nettles.

Brackenbelly desperately reached out for the reins — and missed.

He tumbled from her back.

Fourteen

Isomee pulled off the second drop and flip stunt and faced the right way just as Brackenbelly fell from Bramble's back.

She smiled at the excitement of completing the acrobatic manoeuvre, unaware of her friend's terrible situation. The bolas bounced along at her side, ready for action.

There was no way she was going to throw it at any of her pursuers, though. The odds were she'd miss and then lose the valuable object somewhere in the woods, never to see it again.

If any jakels got close enough, she could swing it down at them and try to hit them.

Isomee glanced over her shoulder to see where her pursuers were. There were no jakels.

And that was when she discovered there was no Brackenbelly either.

Brackenbelly landed on the woodland floor, his pack digging into him. He scattered leaves and crushed saplings as he rolled across the ground.

A fallen tree brought him to a sudden halt as he crashed into it. His head rocked back and hit it, briefly making stars swim before his eyes, and his long, black hair fell out of its top-knot, falling over his face like a curtain.

The plaintive sound of an injured chostri filled Brackenbelly's ears. He blew his hair out of his face and scrambled to his feet.

Bramble had come to a stop a few metres away.

"Oh no," Brackenbelly said.

As the giant bird struggled to walk over to him, Brackenbelly could see she was limping on the same foot she'd hurt earlier.

The uma cursed his carelessness. His reckless actions had hurt Bramble, and if that wasn't bad enough, it could lead to greater disasters if he couldn't escape and find Isomee.

A deep, two-tone growl alerted Brackenbelly that disaster was even closer than he thought. He held his breath and listened. There were four dogs. He could hear them panting and rustling in the undergrowth as they stalked him, slowly coming closer and closer.

Brackenbelly's went to defend himself, but his sword was gone.

He must have dropped it when he fell.

His eyes swept the ground, searching for it.

There!

Sticking up out of the ground, just out of reach between himself and the nearest of the two-headed jakels. It must have slid out of his belt when he fell off Bramble.

Brackenbelly dived for the weapon at the same moment one of the jakels burst from the bushes and charged at him. He landed on the ground and went into a forward roll. As his legs came up over the top they struck the jakel, sending it flying off into the bushes. He finished the roll, ended up back on his feet and pulled the sword out of the ground.

Weapon in hand, Brackenbelly looked to see what had changed since he'd made the dive. The jakels had come out of hiding and were attacking Bramble. It made sense. They could probably tell that she was injured and therefore an easier target.

Brackenbelly rushed towards Bramble, but she was already proving that she was more than capable of looking after herself. The chostri kicked out at the jakel and sent it scurrying off. She then turned to her master and limped toward him.

"Can you still run?" he asked her.

Bramble blinked back at him with wide, unknowing eyes. It was time to try the Chal-Nar again, even if they were in danger. He needed to be able to communicate with her more than ever if there were to get out alive, and more importantly, find Isomee.

Putting his hand on her head, Brackenbelly closed his eyes and said to her, "Find Thorn and Isomee, I'll hold the jakels here."

Brackenbelly opened his eyes again and saw the most wonderful, amazing thing. Bramble bobbed her head up and down three times.

"Quick," he said. "Go!"

He turned from the bird, unable to say goodbye and waited to face the oncoming attackers alone. The sound of Bramble's fleeing steps filled his ears, only to be replaced by the jakel's growls and their faster footfalls.

Brackenbelly prepared himself for the coming attack. It was then that he realised that something was wrong with his sword. He could tell without even looking. He was so used to holding it he could sense it felt lighter.

He looked down at it for the first time.

As he suspected.

The blade was snapped in half.

*

"Brackenbelly?" Isomee called as she pulled on Thorn's reins.

As soon as the chostri stopped she looked back behind her. He was nowhere to be seen.

"Brackenbelly?!" she called again. "Where are you?"

Isomee kicked her ride's side, pulled on the reins and turned Thorn around. He eyed her with a face that seemed to say, *you want me to go back there*?!

"We have to go back. Thorn? Come on, I know you understand me. We need to find Bramble and Brackenbelly."

The chostri wobbled its head from side to side and then started to trot forwards.

"What have you found, boy?"

Thorn sped up and headed to the largest tree in the area and then bent his long neck down.

"What is it?" Isomee said, but the bird ignored her and rooted about in the soft soil at the base of the trunk.

Isomee pulled on the reins.

"Come on! There's nothing there. We have to find Bramble!" Isomee could hear the desperation in her own voice.

A moment later, Thorn's head popped up with an odd looking, orange object in her beak. He squeezed it tight and the thing burst open sending out a jet of sweet smelling juices.

"Food? Is that all you can think about?"

Isomee went quiet. Something was coming through the trees and it sounded as if it were in a hurry. She searched through the bushes and trees, her mouth dry and her heart beat rising.

"Thorn, we need to get moving. They're coming." She pulled on the reins. "Come on, before it's too late."

Thorn moved, but it took all of Isomee's strength to get him to turn his head and face the opposite way from whatever was coming.

A screech filled the air. Isomee looked back over her shoulder. She'd recognise that sound anywhere. It wasn't a jakel. It was a chostri.

Bramble came hurtling around a large bush.

The smile of relief disappeared from Isomee's face.

Brackenbelly wasn't on her.

＊

The four jakels formed a tight circle around Brackenbelly, trapping him as their eight jaws gnashed and ground. Fighting one when he was rescuing Isomee had been hard enough, and that one had only had one head. What were four going to be like?

"I don't want to hurt you," Brackenbelly said, remembering that he had said the same thing the night before to the jakel he had just thought about.

Without any warning, the jakels all charged at once. Brackenbelly bent his knees, ready to spring to action. When they were close enough, he cartwheeled to the right, taking the jakels by surprise. Two of them collided, their thick, heavy skulls cracking together.

The remaining two skidded to a halt and turned to face him.

They were going to be more careful now.

Brackenbelly leapt onto the fallen tree he had hit his head on, quickly tucked the remains of the sword through his belt and ran along it.

The jakels followed, their claws slipping on the smooth wood that had become exposed where the rough bark had fallen off.

Brackenbelly looked back as the sound of their scrambling paws and claws. They were on to him much quicker than he expected. One had its mouth open and was about to take a chunk out of his leg.

Brackenbelly jumped out of the way.

And grabbed the branch above his head. He clambered up into the tree.

"Ha! Missed me," he cried out in triumph.

The jakel below him growled and then jumped into the tangle of lower branches. It scrambled about, trying to get a grip, sending the branch flying around. Finally, it grabbed the branch with one of its mouths.

"Uh, oh," Brackenbelly muttered as he watched what happened next.

The second jakel jumped on top of the first and climbed up over it, onto the main branch.

"That's not good," Brackenbelly said as he stared in wonder as the jakel settled itself and cautiously walked down the branch toward him.

The first jakel let go and fell to the ground, making the tree limb wobble for a moment. It joined the other two and waited patiently below, knowing that their dinner would eventually fall or be knocked down.

Brackenbelly reluctantly drew what was left of his sword, grabbed a branch above his head and steadied himself as the jakel raced toward him.

Fifteen

Brackenbelly kept his eyes fixed on the jakel at the other end of the branch and stamped on his end. It shook, but not enough to shake the jakel loose.

"Nice doggie," Brackenbelly said.

The jakel rolled back its lips and snarled. Drool dripped from its razor-sharp teeth.

"Don't want to be a friend, eh? Look! A bone!" Brackenbelly said and looked away hoping it would copy him.

The jakel snarled.

"Not falling for it, eh? I guess two heads really are better than one."

Brackenbelly stepped back and the double-headed dog jumped at him. The air hissed from Brackenbelly's lungs as the weight of the jakel rammed into him and his foot slipped from the branch. His eyes widened with fear and he reached out to grab something — anything — to stop him falling down to the waiting mouths below. But there was nothing there and he had no choice but to fall.

The forest floor was hard and Brackenbelly's breath hissed through his teeth once again. The other three jakels rushed at him before he even had a chance to get back on his feet. He brought the damaged sword up and, to his surprise, the three growling wild dogs stopped moving.

Brackenbelly wasn't sure if it was the blade that put them off or something else, but he was glad they did.

The fourth jakel jumped down out of the tree and joined the others. They looked at each other for a moment and all started to move together as one.

"I guess that means you're not scared after all," Brackenbelly said and started to crawl backwards.

His only hope was to put some distance between him and the four growling beasts and pray that Bramble came back with Isomee.

And soon.

*

 "Where's Brackenbelly?" Isomee asked the old chostri.

Bramble stopped as soon as she came round the bush and refused to come any closer. Isomee noticed that she seemed to be carrying all her weight on one leg.

"You're hurt. Bramble, tell me, where's Brackenbelly?" Isomee said.

Thorn gulped down the orange fungus he had unearthed and stepped towards his mother. As soon as he did, Bramble turned and started to walk away.

"Do you think she wants us to follow her?" Isomee asked, looking into Thorn's beady eyes. The black orbs stared back at her.

Bramble stopped, let out a high-pitched squawk.

"Brackenbelly must be in trouble," Isomee said. "Come on, let's follow your mum."

*

Brackenbelly moved backwards on his bottom, away from the jakels, one hand at a time. If he did it slowly enough, maybe they wouldn't see that he was getting further away.

The four jakels leaned back, their front legs outstretched before them and brought their heads close to the ground, ready to pounce.

Brackenbelly watched them for a moment longer, bracing himself for the worst fight of his life, and then rushed back as fast as his hands and feet would carry him.

He stopped after a couple of yards.

The jakels stayed exactly where they were.

Brackenbelly was starting to wonder why, when he heard a high pitched whine he instantly recognised.

It was Isomee. Or rather the bolas he'd made for her.

He looked back at the direction the sound was coming from. She was riding Thorn one handed and spinning the bolas above her head. Bramble was limping far behind her.

"So that's it," Brackenbelly said. "You're not so keen now that the odds are more even."

*

Isomee skilfully brought Thorn to a stop behind her friend and carried on twirling the bolas, ready to launch it if she had to.

"Quick, get on. I think Thorn can cope with carrying us both for a short distance," Isomee said.

Brackenbelly didn't reply as he slowly got to his feet, his eyes locked on the four hounds. "They've stopped attacking," he said. "In fact, they've stopped moving towards me."

135

"Good, let's get out of here," Isomee said. "They still look angry to me."

"At first, I thought it was because you'd arrived, but no. There's something more. I can feel it." Brackenbelly said, almost as if he wasn't listening to her. "Let's test it."

Isomee couldn't believe what her friend was saying.

"That's daft. You don't mess about with animals you don't know, especially if they look angry."

"Trust me," Brackenbelly said, reaching out to them.

Isomee couldn't believe her eyes.

One moment they were running in fear and the next Brackenbelly was trying to stroke the very thing they were running from.

To Isomee's amazement, the wild dogs remained silent, but as soon as Brackenbelly moved within an arm's length of them, they started to growl.

He moved back and they went quiet again.

"Interesting," he said.

Isomee heard something behind her, but when she looked it was only Bramble. The poor injured bird had finally caught up with them.

"Bramble's here. Let's go," Isomee said, to Brackenbelly.

"No," he said, and looked back at her. "There's something going on here. I want to try something else."

"What? What's going on?"

Brackenbelly didn't answer as he stepped forward.

The jakels growled.

He stepped back and they stopped again.

"See? There's something going on. Why chase us all this way and stop now, or rather *here*?" Brackenbelly said, pointing at a spot on the floor. "They had me. I couldn't escape, even with your timely arrive."

"It doesn't matter. Brackenbelly, let's just go," Isomee said. She hated this forest. She just wanted to get to Bently. Anywhere where there weren't any dogs that were chasing her.

"I want to know the answer. Don't you? There's only one way to find out," he said and reached out with his hand.

"What are you doing? Are you mad?!" Isomee cried.

"Maybe," said Brackenbelly with a smile.

Isomee wanted to get down from Thorn and pull Brackenbelly away, but she was too scared. She was safe up here and if anything went wrong, she could escape.

Brackenbelly slowly moved his hand forward, spreading his fingers out so that he would look as non-threatening as possible. The jakels continued to growl, quietly, but they still didn't move or act aggressively.

It's like there's an invisible line on the ground that they just can't, or won't, cross, Isomee thought.

Brackenbelly gently placed his hand on top of the lead jakel's head and...

Brackenbelly took his hand away.

"Nothing happened," he said, looking up at Isomee. "I couldn't read their feelings, let alone their thoughts.

It was just like the other one. I've never met an animal where I couldn't at least sense their feelings."

"Well…" Isomee began when the four jakels all started to crawl backwards away from her and Brackenbelly. As soon as they were out of Brackenbelly's striking distance, they turned and ran.

"That was odd," Isomee said as she slid down from Thorn. "Why did they suddenly run away?"

"Yes, it was, and I don't know," Brackenbelly replied in a tone of voice that left Isomee feeling slightly afraid.

Sixteen

Isomee watched the four jakels run off and disappear

into the trees and bushes.

Brackenbelly walked over to Bramble and lifted up

her foot.

"Are you hurt, girl? Don't worry, we'll get you help

soon, I promise."

Isomee took a deep breath and followed him.

"What happened? Why did they suddenly stop?"

she asked.

Brackenbelly put the useless sword through his belt and rubbed his chin, deep in thought.

"Brackenbelly?" Isomee said, this time with more than a hint of frustration in her voice. Why wouldn't he answer her?

"I don't know, but I think if we walk back that way," he said pointing after the dogs, "they'll come after us again."

"Are you saying they just wanted us off their land?"

Brackenbelly nodded, but Isomee couldn't help but think he had another idea that he didn't want to share with her.

"I think we should set up camp for the night. There's still hours of sunlight left but Bramble needs to rest that foot," Brackenbelly said.

"Are you sure we'll be safe here?"

"Yes," he answered.

Isomee looked at him. In the short time she'd known him, Brackenbelly had only ever been honest with her and looked out for her safety. She was probably worrying about nothing.

"Good," she said.

"You stay here with Bramble and Thorn. I'll have a quick scout around for somewhere safe to stay."

"I saw a steaming dragon duct not far from here as I raced back to save you. I think the water inside's warm, and I could do with a bath," Isomee paused for a moment, sniffed and added, "and so could you."

Brackenbelly stared at her and said, "Uma only have one bath a year."

"Really?"

"No, I'm kidding. After what we've been through, I think a nice relaxing soak would be good for the muscles, don't you? You're not afraid of it, are you?"

"The dragon duct? No. Why would I be?" Isomee asked.

"After what happened last night, I wouldn't be surprised."

"Well, that wasn't the dragon duct's fault, was it? And at least this one won't be freezing cold."

"Let's give it a quick look over, though, just to be safe."

Brackenbelly took Bramble's reins and led her in the direction Isomee had pointed to.

"Wait a minute, Brackenbelly," she said. "There something I've got to ask. What happened to your sword? And what *is* going on with your hair?" Isomee asked with a smile.

The uma looked up at his loose hair. Isomee was sure she saw him blush.

"It came loose. I must do it back up."

Isomee thought that was an interesting thing to say. She wanted to ask him more about it, but perhaps now was not the time.

They set off, putting more distance between themselves and the jakels. Brackenbelly was silent the whole way and Isomee was left wondering what had made the wild-dogs stop. What wasn't Brackenbelly telling her?

In the distance, Isomee spotted wisps of steam.

"There it is," she said, pointing.

When they got to it, the dragon duct was huge and almost completely full to the brim with water.

"This looks good," Brackenbelly said, smiling for the first time in ages.

Isomee crouched down at the edge.

"What I like best is that it's so full, even if I fall in, I'll be able to climb out again."

Brackenbelly laughed.

"That wasn't a joke!" Isomee said.

"Oh," Brackenbelly said as he dipped his hands into the warm water, disturbing the steam as well as the surface.

"It must be safe. Look," Isomee said pointing out into the centre of the pool. Fish were swimming in it.

Before they got too comfortable, Isomee and Brackenbelly gathered enough wood for the night. Then they collected edible berries and roots. Isomee knew that once she sat down she wouldn't want to get back up.

Once the camp was all organised, they checked on Bramble and Thorn. Bramble's foot didn't look that bad, a little swollen, but Brackenbelly felt sure that it would go down by morning and she would be fit for travel, even if he had to walk beside her.

"I think I'll have that bath now," Isomee said.

"All right," said Brackenbelly. "I'll go back to where the jakels left us. I'll leave Bramble here with you. If anything happens while I'm away, take both Thorn and Bramble and get out of here. Understand?"

"Yes. Do you expect any more trouble?" she asked, her eyes flicking about wildly, looking for something.

Brackenbelly placed his hands on her shoulders.

"No. Not at all. Now, enjoy your bath."

By the time he returned an hour later, Isomee was sat by the fire combing her red hair with her fingers.

"Find anything?" she said.

"No."

"Go and have your bath. I'll make dinner using the roots and berries we found."

When Brackenbelly returned, his hair tied up once again, they ate.

It started to get dark and soon the light of the fire started to make Isomee feel safe and relaxed. She grabbed a piece of silver birch branch and peeled off its bark. Then she plucked a twig out of the fire and blew out the flaming end. Once it was cool, Isomee flattened out the piece of narrow bark and started scratching on the inside of it with the stick.

The pair fell into silence as Isomee went about her work.

"What are you doing?" Brackenbelly asked after some time had passed.

Isomee held up the bark for him to see what she had been doing. It was a picture.

"I thought I'd draw maps of our adventures. What do you think?"

Brackenbelly smiled at her.

"You're good at drawing."

"I'd like to write our adventures down but," Isomee turned away from Brackenbelly before adding, "but I don't know how to. How to write, I mean. Uncle never taught me."

"A picture paints a thousand words," Brackenbelly said kindly.

"Can you read and write, Brackenbelly?"

The uma nodded.

"Would you teach me?" Isomee asked.

Brackenbelly smiled and nodded.

"Of course, I will. On one, very important condition."

"Anything. I'd do anything. I'll practise really hard, I'll…"

"Isomee, calm down. It's nothing like that. I'll teach you to read and write if you teach me to draw."

Isomee stopped and stared at him. She couldn't believe her ears.

"Deal," Isomee said happily as she packed away her makeshift paper, lay down beside the fire and covered herself with his cloak.

"First, we needed clothes, boots, and a new sword," Brackenbelly said. "Now we need to add paper and ink to the shopping list. Things are going to get expensive when we get to Bently."

"I can stay in this dress a little longer if it helps," Isomee said.

"No," Brackenbelly smiled. "We'll be all right. I probably have enough money. And if need be, we'll get some work."

"Goodnight, Bracken," she said, feeling comfortable and happy around another person for the first time in her life.

"Goodnight, Isomee."

Her mouth opened to say something, but her eyelids fell shut as if the weight of the day had finally got too much. Without saying another word, she fell asleep.

*

Isomee felt her body being shaken.

Her eyes flickered open again.

"Is it time to get up already?" she said, thinking Brackenbelly was shaking her.

She sat up and leaned back on her arms. It was still dark and Brackenbelly was fast asleep on the other side of the fire.

What had woken her?

"I must have been drea—"

Isomee stopped talking. Something *was* shaking, and it wasn't her. She could feel the movement through the palms of her hands.

The ground was shaking.

Isomee blinked, looked towards the edge of the duct and then straight back at Brackenbelly.

Something huge was inside the swirling steam from the dragon duct.

Seventeen

Isomee stared into the steam, trying to make out whatever it was that was hiding within it.

A huge, lumbering shape disturbed the swirling vapour as it climbed out of the pool, sending a wave of water up over the side.

It reminded Isomee of a snake she had once found hiding at the back of the barn. It had been a very savage winter and the poor thing was taking shelter.

Her uncle had sent her away on some errand and killed it while she wasn't around to protest it.

But the thing climbing out of the water was also nothing like a snake. It had four short legs and a pair of small wings. Its body was much, much shorter than a snake's, and it was wider than the fattest pig back on Hogg-Bottom farm.

Isomee stared, unable to move as the beast opened its mouth and out came a giant forked tongue.

*

Brackenbelly awoke when the water tumbled over the lip of the duct. He was on his feet with the broken sword in his hand before the creature had climbed out of the pool.

"Load up the chostri, get away from here," he said to Isomee as he ran away from the fire and towards the lumbering beast.

This was exactly what he was afraid of and why he hadn't shared his thoughts with Isomee hours earlier.

Those jakels had stopped for a reason, and the reason was that there was something bigger and more scary than them.

Brackenbelly ran towards the dragon duct and skidded to a halt. He looked back at his pack and thought about what was inside it, wrapped in the delicate red fabric. He could use it, perhaps he *should* use it, but he wouldn't.

Not today.

*

"Wait!" Isomee shouted at Brackenbelly as she groggily threw back the cloak, shook off the remains of her short sleep, snatched a burning branch out of the fire and ran after him.

There was no way she was going to let him face that thing on his own.

"What are we going to do?" she asked as she came to a stop beside him.

Brackenbelly didn't answer, he simply held out his arm to stop her going any further.

"We can't fight it. We need to escape while we still have the chance."

The beast lumbered forward. It moved much faster than Isomee expected, considering its size. Its body alone was as big as her uncle, and then there was the tail added on the end.

"Get back," Brackenbelly yelled. "And run like I told you. Don't worry, I'm coming too. Even I'm not going to take this on."

Isomee turned and ran back to the camp. The sound of Brackenbelly's footsteps not far behind her.

The whole ground suddenly heaved beneath her feet, sending Isomee tumbling to the ground, her head narrowly missing the circle of stones which they had made to contain the fire,

She looked back to see what had happened. The giant lizard was now fully out of the water and closing in on them. With alarming speed, the beast turned and its tail snapped around like a whip and swept Brackenbelly off his feet.

*

Brackenbelly dropped to the hard rock beneath him.

He didn't wait before he acted. If he hesitated, it would be the end.

He dashed past the creature's gnashing mouth and grabbed the reptile's tail in the crook of his left arm. He stabbed the ragged end of his sword at it but the broken weapon glanced uselessly off the armoured scales. Brackenbelly watched in horror as it slid down the skin and narrowly missed his own leg by the thickness of a chostri's claw.

"We don't stand a chance against a… a… a…" Brackenbelly was unable to say the word.

It couldn't be one, could it?

With a powerful flick of its tail, the beast threw Brackenbelly off. He sailed through the air and crashed into a tree. He seemed to stay there for a moment, pinned to the trunk, before he fell to the ground, dropping his sword.

*

Isomee curled up next to the fire and clamped her hands over her ears as Thorn let out two shrill shrieks. The young chostri clambered to his feet and rushed forward.

"Where are you going?" Isomee called, but Thorn didn't stop.

The chostri stopped in front of the lizard and made a vicious peck at its eye. It turned its head to avoid the swipe and opened its mouth, revealing rows of teeth designed to crush and rip, and let out a loud roar.

Isomee looked around the darkened trees. If there was anything still asleep in the forest, it wasn't now. Maybe something would come and help them.

More likely they'd run away.

By the time Isomee turned her attention back to her faithful chostri, Bramble had joined her son in the attack.

With a screeching, biting, kicking bird on either side of its head, the dragon had no choice but to move back. The two brave chostri chased it further away from Isomee and the fire, driving it back toward the dragon duct.

As the dragon's tail dipped back into the water, Thorn retreated back toward Isomee.

The moment he left Bramble on her own, the dragon attacked her. The chostri smoothly hopped back out of the way but landed heavily on her injured ankle. Bramble's leg collapsed below her.

"No!" Isomee called, as she started to get back up to help her.

Before Isomee had even taken a step, the dragon, seeing its opportunity, surged forward like a relentless wave toward the helpless bird, its mouth open wide, ready to attack.

*

Brackenbelly screamed, "You leave her alone!"

He'd been busy while the two chostri had the beast's attention. Far from laying on the floor nursing his wounds, he'd found a vine and a head-sized stone and tied the two together.

He charged towards the giant lizard and swung the rock on the end of the rope like a giant bolas made from just one rope.

The reptile turned its head and lashed its tail out at Brackenbelly, but this time, he was prepared. He somersaulted over the living weapon, landed beside the creature and leapt onto its shoulders.

With both ends of the vine in his right hand, he threw the end with the stone under the beast's head as hard as he could. It swung under the neck and curved back up towards his other waiting hand. His three fingers grabbed the vine and he quickly wrapped the slack on both ends around his palms. Taking a deep breath, and hoping his plan would work, he pulled the vine tight around the beast's neck.

The giant lizard tried to roar in anger, but the vine was digging into its throat. It thrashed from side to side and stomped its tail on the ground as it tried to throw Brackenbelly off its back.

But he held on tight and pulled and pulled with all his might as he rode the unsteady overgrown reptile.

*

Isomee watched Brackenbelly ride the giant reptile for a moment and then got to her feet. She ran past Thorn to his fallen mother.

"Come on, Bramble. Let's get out of here and let Brackenbelly take care of this," Isomee said as she placed her arm over the top of the bird's body and patted her encouragingly.

Thorn trotted up and squawked at his mother. The three retreated as quickly as they could, careful to keep out of range of the struggling dragon as Brackenbelly rode it.

When she knew both chostri were safe, Isomee turned to look back at Brackenbelly and the enormous lizard. She watched as the reptile suddenly sprung up into the air, beating its undersized-wings, with Brackenbelly still valiantly clinging onto its back.

Her mouth hung open in amazement as the beast's tiny wings somehow held the enormous lizard in the air. Then it altered direction and the force of the draft created by the wings battered Isomee, lifting her off her feet.

Leaves and twigs swirled in the air, as the dragon continued to fly, forcing Isomee to protect her face. Through a gap in her arms, Isomee saw that Thorn and Bramble had tucked their heads under their wings and fallen to the floor, keeping themselves as small as possible and protecting their own eyes.

Isomee heard the wings make a loud flap.

Then the draft stopped.

Isomee uncovered her eyes just in time to see the dragon twist in the air, dive down into the steaming water and disappear.

"No!" she screamed.

Isomee began to get to her feet when the dragon burst back out of the water and hovered over the pool of water.

"Oh no!" Isomee called.

Brackenbelly was no longer sitting on its back.

Eighteen

Isomee stood up and stared, first at the formidable creature above the pool and then at the water. She wanted to run forward and dive in to save Brackenbelly, but something was stopping her.

Her eyes shot back up to the flying lizard — was it a dragon? — as it hovered above the pool, its tail slapping the water as it swung lazily from side to side.

With a sudden twist and a powerful beat of its wings, the dragon rose up into the air, flew toward

Isomee and then folded its wings along its body. The heavy, armoured beast crashed to the ground, knocking her off her feet as the earth shook beneath her.

Isomee quickly got up and rushed back to the fire and picked up a burning branch. The dragon thundered across the ground towards the fire, towards her, towards the chostri. Her legs trembled beneath her. She wanted to run.

The dragon stopped in front of her.

Without thinking, Isomee thrust the flaming stick at the creature's face. It moved back, fleeing the heat of the flames.

"It came out of the water," Isomee shouted. "It doesn't like fire. Brackenbelly, it doe…."

Isomee didn't finish her sentence. How had she forgotten he was no longer there to hear her? It was going to be up to her to use the knowledge she had gained to save herself and get away with the chostri.

Maybe it wouldn't be too late to save her friend as well.

The dragon charged forward, taking Isomee by surprise. It lashed out with one of its stunted legs and knocked the flaming branch out of her hand.

Isomee screamed as it flew from her grasp and landed a few yards away.

Her theory about the fire had been wrong, and now she had no way of defending herself. She'd seen what had happened to Brackenbelly. Even the chostri seemed to have given up trying to fight the massive beast.

It was hopeless.

She turned away and looked behind her. She should escape while she had the chance. Maybe it would be too large to get through the trees. If she escaped she should go back home. Uncle Hogg-Bottom might be cruel, but at least she'd be safe there.

Isomee crawled backwards, trying to put as much space as she could between herself and the dragon, but it lumbered after her, slowly and confidently as if it knew that it had defeated them all.

The beast moved faster and Isomee's eyes widened with fear as it walked over the top of her, its legs straddling her body. She should have got back to her feet, then she wouldn't be trapped underneath it.

It was too late now. She could feel its huge body pressing down upon her, squashing her. She tried to scream but there was no air in her lungs. Isomee began to panic and in one last desperate attempt to free herself, she pushed against the dragon's chest with her hands.

It was no good. She wasn't strong enough.

She was going to...

A sharp pain flashed through Isomee's body. Her mind was filled with a bright, agonising light. At first, she thought the dragon had finally crushed her, but it was something else. It felt as if lightning was flooding through her, like she was charged with energy. Then, Isomee found she had air in her lungs to scream.

So she did.

She screamed as loud as she could, as loud as she ever had, as she pushed against the scaled skin with her hands.

Then the crushing weight was gone.

The pain was gone too.

Confused, Isomee opened her eyes.

The dragon was tumbling away from her, twisting through the air as if something had thrown or pushed it away from her.

Isomee felt a tingling in her fingers and when she looked at her hands, her eyes grew wide with fear and amazement. Energy, like tiny streaks of lightning, rippled on the ends of her fingers and up her arms.

The dragon roared and Isomee forgot about her fingers and looked at the huge, flying reptile. Somehow it had managed to control its tumble and brought itself to a standstill. The dragon hovered in the air for a moment and with a powerful swipe of its wings, charged back at her.

Isomee froze as the dragon opened its vicious cave-like mouth and came at her. In a feeble attempt to protect herself, she threw her hands up as if she could make it stop.

The last of the energy in her fingers crackled and released itself as a powerful blast of screaming air came from her hands and smashed into the dragon. The violent blast made the beast wobble in the air like a kite in a sudden, unexpected gust of wind. The unexplained power didn't stop the creature, but it did slow it down.

Isomee stared at her fingers again, but didn't feel afraid anymore. She knew what had happened to her. She had been granted a Lak-Ti. If she used it cleverly and correctly, it would give her the power to take care of the dragon and get Bramble and Thorn to safety.

Maybe there would even be time to save Brackenbelly.

Isomee went into a forward roll, came up into a sitting position, put her hands up on either side of her head and flicked them forward, somehow instinctively knowing how to use her new found powers.

Another devastating blast of howling air shot out from her fingertips leaving a vortex of wind trailing behind it, sucking up leaves and debris. The blast smashed into the dragon, knocking it to one side and back over the top of the steaming dragon duct.

Still the power was not enough. The huge lizard regained its balance and looked at its prey as it hovered. Isomee thought that once, not so long ago, it looked at her as a tasty morsel, but now she was sure she saw fear in its eyes.

The dragon twisted in the air, dived down into the water and...

Isomee waited for it to come back. She counted to thirty by counting three lots of ten, just like Brackenbelly had taught her.

But the dragon didn't come back.

Isomee rushed to the edge of the pool. The water sloshed around inside the huge pit and up over the side. Bracing herself for a surprise attack, she waited for the surface of the water to calm back down. When the water finally settled, the dragon was nowhere to be seen.

Isomee smiled for a moment and the feeling of triumph was instantly replaced by sadness as she realised that it was not the only thing that hadn't come back up.

Brackenbelly was nowhere to be seen in the steaming water, and that could only mean one thing.

Numb, Isomee stood and stared for a while before she sat on the edge of the dragon duct and cried.

The two chostri came and sat one on either side of her.

Tears streamed down her face as the sadness of her loss reminded her of the last time it had happened. Everyone she'd loved or cared about died, and this time, she was old enough to fully understand and remember.

Bramble rubbed her soft cheek on Isomee's, trying to wipe away her tears.

"I…" she started to say, but Isomee couldn't find the words she wanted. She sniffed, wiped away her tears and sat in silence for a moment with both of the chostri's heads on her shoulders.

The forest suddenly felt very quiet.

In the distance, Isomee thought she heard a muffled bark. Her heart quickened at the thought of being attacked by the doubled-headed jakels again. She had her own Lak-Ti now, but she feared that against multiple targets it wouldn't be of any use.

The bark came again and Isomee listened more carefully. While she didn't know much about jakels, she understood animals. The barking didn't sound angry or aggressive. It sounded insistent, like there was something urgent it needed her to know.

Isomee leapt to her feet.

It was coming from the pool.

Looking out across the steamy water, Isomee saw a brown shape moving towards her. She peered through the blanket of mist, desperate to see what.

A jakel was swimming towards her — a jakel with only one head and stripe down its back.

As it got closer, Isomee saw a vine clamped tightly in its mouth. It was dragging a dark shape behind it.

Isomee's heart raced even though she tried not to raise her hopes.

As the jakel got closer, Isomee couldn't contain herself any longer and she dived into the warm water.

"Thank you, thank you," she said to the jakel as she swam past it and up to the precious thing it had rescued.

It was Brackenbelly.

∩ineteen

Isomee swam back to the edge of the dragon duct,

grateful she could easily climb out this time.

She turned round and watched as Brackenbelly's body floated to the edge. The one-headed jakel jumped out and shook itself dry as Isomee grabbed the shoulder of Brackenbelly's tunic and pulled.

He was unconscious and too heavy.

"Help me!" she pleaded the three animals. The jakel manoeuvred its jaw until it was able to grip Brackenbelly's clothes. The chostri wiggled their heads and necks under his arms. Together, they lifted Brackenbelly out of the water and back onto dry land.

"Quick, let's get him to the fire," Isomee said even though she knew they wouldn't understand her.

The team of four moved the uma over to the heat of the fire. Isomee unwound the vine from his hands, threw his cloak over him and added more wood to the fire.

Bramble used her wings to blow air on the fire and her son soon copied her.

Isomee sat and waited, just as he had done for her the night before, and bit her nails. Bramble and Thorn cuddled up next to each other and the jakel curled up at Isomee's feet.

The sun was beginning to come through the trees but Isomee's eyelids were too heavy to hold open any longer. Slowly, her head sagged against her chest until she fell asleep.

*

Isomee was awoken by Brackenbelly coughing.

"What happened?" he said, getting up from the ground where she had made his bed.

Isomee put her hand on his shoulder and gently pushed him back down.

"You need to rest."

"What…?" he started saying.

"You were saved," she began, "by…"

The jakel, who had stayed by Brackenbelly's feet the whole time he was asleep, got up and licked his face.

Brackenelly instantly sat back up.

"You're alive," Brackenbelly said, his face filled with joy and wonder.

"We're *all* alive!" Isomee said in triumph. "I thought I'd lost you. What happened?"

"The dragon dragged me down into the water and then stopped. The next thing I knew, I was sinking because of the heavy rock on the end of the vine. I was just about to unwrap it from my hands when I saw something heading up through the water toward me. It was a fish."

"A fish?" Isomee asked.

Brackenbelly nodded.

"Before my very eyes it turned into this jakel," he said, giving the wild dog a friendly rub on the head. "It chewed through the vine and the rock fell way. Then it grabbed the vine in its mouth and it started bringing me back up. We were almost at the surface when the dragon re-entered the pool and came swimming past us. We were both caught in its current and dragged back down. I thought I was going to die but I was more afraid that I was too late to save you. Obviously, you didn't need me," he said smiling at her.

"I do need you," she said kindly. "And I would have been killed if it hadn't happened."

"What? What happened?" the uma asked, confused.

"Remember how I asked if only uma could be a... what did you call them again? The special people, I mean."

"Fal-Muru?" Brackenbelly suggested. "The Chosen?"

"Yes, them. Remember I asked if only uma could be Fal-Muru and have a Lak-Ti?"

"Yes."

"Well, the answer's no," Isomee said, holding up her hands.

"What do you mean? What happened? How?" Brackenbelly asked.

"I was trapped under the dragon and I tried to push it away. I knew it was pointless, it was far too heavy, but I was desperate. I guess that was when it happened, just like when you were bitten. It was my life or death moment that unlocked my power. I was filled with a kind of lightning energy. It's all gone now. I haven't tried my powers since. Maybe they were just temporary."

Brackenbelly sat and stared for a while and said, "That's normal. The energy is just what sparks the birth of your power. You'll still have it, I'm sure. What is it?"

"I can shoot blasts of air from my hands."

"Interesting."

"Interesting?" Isomee said, not believing Brackenbelly's less than enthusiastic response. "It was awesome! Hang on," Isomee said pointing at the jakel, "did you say he was a fish?"

"He can change shape — become anything he wants — so maybe that makes three of us," Brackenbelly said, giving the jakel another rub on the head and stroking its ears.

"Three?"

"Yes. He must be a Fal-Maru, too. I told you, the Lak-Ti is always linked to the life-threatening danger you were facing. He couldn't breathe underwater so he changed into something that could."

"But last night it attacked you."

"I know, but I did try to save it. My Lak-Ti didn't work on him, but perhaps it worked enough for him to know my intentions. Maybe he was returning the favour. For some reason, I can't create a Chal-Nar with him, but I'll keep on trying. Maybe now he has his own gift, it'll be possible. I'll get some answers, but it seems happy enough to be with us now, don't you think?"

Isomee nodded as Brackenbelly hugged the jakel while it licked his hands.

"Are we going to move on?" she asked.

"Why? Are you in a rush?" Brackenbelly asked. Isomee shook her head. "Besides, nothing else can happen today, surely?"

"No, I suppose not," Isomee smiled.

"I don't know about you, but I need a few days off. And you look exhausted," Brackenbelly said.

"I stayed up all night watching over you, but now I'm too happy to sleep."

"Well, we could get moving and do the shopping we need in Bently, or…"

"Or what?"

"Or we could add some writing to your maps," Brackenbelly said.

"But…" Isomee began and then smiled excitedly at her friend. "Does that mean…"

"Yes, let's start your first lesson. I've a feeling there's going to be lots of new things for you to learn."

Brackenbelly and Isomee return in...

Out now!

Acknowledgements

This story would not have been possible without the considerable help, support and advice from many people. Of those, I would like to send special thanks to Sally, Louise, Elene, but most of all, Nichola and William, my son.

About The Author

For 20 years Gareth Baker has been a primary school teacher, educating and inspiring children across the UK. Gareth's own childhood left him forever fascinated with heroes and their path of discovery and greatness. This is thanks to such films as Star Wars and The Three Musketeers. For most of his youth, Gareth grew up in the countryside on farms all over England because his father was a shepherd. Today, Gareth lives in a world of his own, along with his family, with superhero comics, books, films and computer games. He likes to deliberately say words wrong, plays the violin, the ukulele and Singstar.

He looks forward to sharing his next story with you soon.

Also Available

To save the future he must become a hero from the past

TIME
GUARDIANS
THE MINOTAUR'S ECLIPSE
Gareth Baker

Race into the future of gaming

Also

Available

Please visit

www.gareth-baker.com

for more information

games

videos

and lots more

Sign up for the

Gareth Baker

Newsletter

and get all the latest news

Please try and find some time to visit
Amazon and write a review of this book.